Love, Me and Bullshit!

One man's dream, others' nightmare

Love, Me and Bullshit!

One man's dream, others' nightmare

Vivek Kumar Agarwal

Srishti
PUBLISHERS & DISTRIBUTORS

Srishti Publishers & Distributors
N-16, C. R. Park
New Delhi 110 019
srishtipublishers@gmail.com

First published by Srishti Publishers & Distributors in 2012

2nd impression, 2012

All characters in this book are fictitious, and any resemblance to real persons, living or dead, is coincidental.

Typeset in AGaramond 12pt. by Suresh Kumar Sharma at Srishti

Printed and bound in India

Dedicated to,

The lion I didn't chase

(With this, I consider our karma settled)

Acknowledgement

This story underwent a prolonged and painful birthing process to happen. It had long been cooking without ever getting cooked. Over time, I built my defenses for not being able to write it. With the IIM fabric running through my story, I told myself that I did not want to write another IIM story. I did not want to be another IIM boy writing about the IIMs. Then came a time when I began to lose interest in things around me. The idea of this story kept returning to me like an anchor rope to a sinking ship. But I didn't know how to catch it. I didn't know where to start. I didn't know how to write. For inspiration, I looked at other similar campus stories. I bought a few. Just released, 'Two states' being one of them. I went through it grudgingly. Like anyone even remotely to do with books or a book-shop, I too had an opinion about its writer. Not a very favourable one. I hoped to find reasons to further support my opinion. As I rummaged through it pages, it made me laugh. And occasionally gripped me. Opinions are seldom unbiased. Laughter never has any basis. It just is. I also discovered what I was looking for. The right tone of delivery for my story.

It took a post midnight panic-stricken mental wreckness of couple of hours to enable me to write. Then it kept coming. Trickling, pouring, stuttering. Many people, events, and acts filled in the space between these trickles and downpours. Notable among these are a set of Monkey and Orangutan who shared with me many a meals and cuppa of tea as after having emptied myself on the pages, I waited my cup of ideas to be filled in again.

Below is my brief list of acknowledgements.

Chetan: For getting me started

The Moneky and Orangutan: For helping me sustain

The story itself: For helping me sail through

Thank you.

The Prologue

Scene 1: Midnight

Inner voice (Frustrated): I need a new idea. My mind has become blocked. What's the quickest way to clear it.

Master voice (Doped): Go jump from somewhere. On your way down, everything will become clear.

Inner voice (Still frustrated): Jump from where?

Master voice (More doped): Kutub Minar may be.

I left and jumped from Kutub Minar. The Master voice was right. It always is. My mind was instantly clear. 'Bachaaaooo,' I screamed.

Scene 2: No idea

I: Who am I? Where am I? Who are you?

They: You are an idiot. You are in Angel land. We are Angels.

I: How did I reach here?

They: You jumped from Kutub Minar. Hitting one of us. Why did you do that? You have nothing better to do?

I: Actually not.

They: Why? Why not write that story you been thinking about?

I: Oh, that IIM story. There already are fifty around it.

They: Let there be fifty one then. How does it matter?

Blackout

To all the naysayers, I have permission from higher up. What to do? I went to IIMA, so I can only write about it. Fuck you. Amen.

1
MY ENVY, OTHER'S PRIDE

I felt depressed. "Puneet has received calls from all the six IIMs," Rupali told over breakfast. This was my fourth and last attempt at belling the CAT. Puneet's calls were making my sense of failure acute. I felt like I had a chance too. *May be I hadn't prepared enough. Puneet isn't any better. So the feeling I always have, of losing by a close margin is true.* Last night, Puneet, Rupali, and I had gone out for dinner.

"Bhediye, are the CAT results out?" asked Puneet.

"Of course. You don't know? It has been more than two weeks since they have been out," I replied.

"Is it? Did you check yours? What happened?"

"*Abe*, if I had got a call would I have been sitting with you here? I would have been in seventh heaven. I don't need to check results since I know I don't stand a chance. I have fucked up my paper. And, if I was selected I would have received the courier from them, the same applies to you as well."

"Oh, but I had given the address of my home town, Satara. I haven't called my parents in the last couple of weeks."

"But wouldn't they have told you if a courier had come?"

"No, they are not educated enough to understand what is what. They keep all my posts at one place for me to check whenever I go home unless I enquire about something in particular."

"Oh."

His open response made me close within. It seemed that Puneet and I shared more than just a casual friendship and common workplace. He seemed to belong to a similar background as mine and had similar desires. The difference was that he was cool with it while I felt embarrassed talking about my parents and wore this happy-go-lucky demeanour. He was intelligent but whacky and didn't seem to have the panache and wit that I had, or so I thought. But overnight everything had changed between Puneet and me. He had got what I had once desperately aspired for.

I stared at my computer. *So, will have to continue being a software engineer, which is not bad but now would know that I could have had a better chance but maybe didn't try hard enough.* It didn't matter if I could or could not have done anything better, failure is failure and no explanation helps.

Sanno noticed me sitting with my head low and came up to the cubicle.

"What happened?"

"Nothing, just like that. Not feeling good."

His eyes told me that I can't lie to him. "Okay, Puneet got IIM interview calls. It is just making me feel bad about myself."

"But you had hardly prepared for it this year. I thought you were not interested in it anymore. You were talking about a job switch or doing business or something last time."

"I know, and I really don't care. I haven't even checked my results as I have fucked the paper anyway. But somehow I don't like not getting selected, now that Puneet has got selected."

"Hmmm, give a call to Garima. You would be fine."

"No *yaar*, I am not sure. My heart is really not into her. Sometimes I like her, at others I am not sure."

"Fuck your heart. So what if you were not able to bell this CAT, go and bell the other one," he said and winked, making me smile.

"And this time, don't be shy, okay." Giving a broad smile he pushed my mobile into my hand. Feeling a little better, I called up Garima. I plugged one earpiece while the other one was used by Sanno. He was my luv-guru and I needed his advice at critical moments.

"Hey, how are you," she said, sounding upbeat.

"Good, listen I was wondering if we can meet today evening."

"Today? No, not possible. Lotsa work."

"Come on, please." Sanno had told earlier that one has to insist with girls.

"No, not happening. Fish, my boss is here, will call you later."

"Please, I am missing you." Sanno typed on my computer as I said them over the phone.

"What? What did you just say?"

"Nothing."

"Say it again and I might come."

"Repeat," typed Sanno. I objected and made a bad face.

"I am missing you, what else! Why do you have to make me say it again and again?"

I could sense her smile over the call. "Okay, I would come but you will have to pick me up from the square. Okay?"

"Sure. What time?"

"Around six?"

"Hundred percent. See you in the evening then. Will give you a call to check."

"Okay, byee."

Sanno felt pleased at his pupil's progress. He patted my back, wished me good luck and left for his seat. I got lost in thoughts about a disappointing past, confused present, and a rosy future.

2

FLASHBACK: DOWN THE LANE

Self-reflective thoughts had begun to storm my mind. It had been a few years since I had been chasing the dream called IIM. *Quite strange a chase for a guy like me, really.* Back home, knew no one who wanted to get there. IAS was the thing. An ambassador with a blue light, a crore in dowry, and a lifetime of power over relatives and friends. What more could one want! Oh, and you get a palatial bungalow to live in filled with umpteen servants; some for work, most for show. What a kingly life I say. During the summer break, post our Board exams, me and friends would wander off near to the DM bungalow and wonder, "how does it feel to be inside the bungalow?" That is all we did mostly. Wander about. Not many places to wander really in that small city of ours. *And what were our favourite joints? Ah, yes, the railway station and the bus station.* DM bungalow was not really in our "go to" list but it was close to the girls' college, another of our favourite haunts. Waiting for the college to get over, we would park our bicycles outside the DM Bungalow. Suddenly the gate would open and an ambassador would go past making us wonder, *how would it feel to be in that car?* Disgusting, is what I always thought. And more importantly boring.

"There is just too much responsibility. And it's just too murky. Corruption. Politicians. Not at all cool," said I. Okay, would not have used word "cool". It had just one meaning back then, cold. But had said something to that effect.

"*Abe*, who asked you to work. And who asked you to ask for money. We will do that on your behalf. You just get in there once," said Sudhir.

"Really *dost*. If anyone amongst us can get there, it is you," added Khan.

"*Haan bhaiya*. He is a topper." Sudhir tapped on my head. I grinned. I was a bit irritated. Girls came to my rescue. I mean girls of the local girls' College. The College had just got over and they had begun to run past on their bicycles. Everyone got busy ogling at them leaving me in peace for a few moments. I knew at that moment what I wanted in life. Girls. To be in the girls' place I mean. I wanted to be looked at the way my friends were looking at them. Oh, don't get me wrong, I don't swing the other way. Just wanted to be in the limelight, I mean. How to get there was something that I had to figure out. *Had seen a shooting star that evening. Tried making a wish but couldn't. Didn't know about IIMs. Nor had any wish. 'Damn!' If only I knew.*

Sudhir, Khan, and I. Huh and huh! Don't even think of them much now. Crazy, cruel life. Or just fast running me. They did use to hint that I would drift away from them. Wonder why they said so. Used to get angry. Would fight and make emotional speeches. About living, fucking, and dying together. Middle part obviously with different partners. *How far have we wandered away from each other in our wanderings! I am thinking of them now because my dream has been shattered. Searching them on the streets I deserted long ago. Isn't it a good thing, this shattering of dreams for it brings you back to people who really matter?* Philosophical musings.

Escape mechanism, I tell you. If I somehow got a call from IIM, would dump all the twenty Khans of my life and run after it.

Knowing about IIM would not have helped. It would have remained a faraway dream I didn't even know the meaning of 'fuck' and 'prostitute' when I was seventeen. Definitely knew their Hindi version though. Come on! Not that one needs to know these words to crack CAT. But it reveals how good I was with English. Came to know of my ignorance during a quiz conducted in the engineering class around our vocabulary about the THE THING. Had declined to participate for it was way below my morals. Was silently trying to answer every word in my head though. I had not been able to answer for these two words and had later checked in the English to Hindi dictionary. And then I met Sushant. He changed my life forever. I believe in angels. Yeah, I do. I really do. We shared many things together. Dreams of making it big without knowing the definition of big. Lust and curiosity for a metro-urban life. He told me about CAT. About IIMs. About life in it. About life after it. Money. Glamour. Girls. We would roam around the city on my bicycle feasting on tea and sweets. One winter afternoon we decided to visit the nearby zoo. On the warm afternoons on a weekday only two kinds of people visit the zoo. Couples with no other place to hide, and eve-teasers with no other place to find the couples. We belonged to the latter group. Isn't that obvious? But that day there were no couples. There were deer. Roaming around in open! When God takes a snake from you, he offers you a lizard, goes the timeless proverb. Sushant looked upwards, trying to figure out what was God wanting us to do. He was an Angel. It was a sign. I didn't know how to look for them. Signs I mean. I still don't. When you have a direct connect with him, you get His message in a jiffy. "Let us chase the deer. It will strengthen our legs," Sushant told me. I agreed. We ran towards them from opposite ends, hoping to catch them. But damn quick they are I tell you. Would quickly scatter around and we would have to wait for over fifteen minutes before they gathered back. I don't like waiting. I was a King in my last birth actually. It's a habit I am unable to relinquish. We decided to enter the cage and chase them there. Where would they run from us inside a cage? To up the challenge we chose Chinkaras, who had shapely, long antlers. We assessed the target and decided that they are harmless so we could harm them. But we couldn't. Compared to them we were snails. We kept changing corners but it didn't help. "It is time to change the strategy," I said. "Let's enter the lion's cage. Lions are not that fast. He won't be able to run away," I advised. Sushant stared. He was dumb. It always took him time to get the ideas.

"Are you nuts. You can't do it."

It wasn't his fault. He had never been the believer. His convictions were always weak. I persisted.

"I am telling you it's the Cheetah, which is quick. Lions are lazy. And the ones in the zoo are dead meat, man. Can't run to save their lives."

But he wouldn't agree. He was quite adamant at times. I don't like that trait in people. But I still gave in. What to do? Friendship needs sacrifices. What would he know. Picking up our bicycle we reached for the tea shop. Fulli Bhai took over fifteen minutes to deliver his tea. We waited, ogling at the girls in the vicinity. Not our fault. All because Fulli wouldn't give us the tea quickly. It is strange that people do not realize how their seemingly perfectionist tendencies are damaging the world in more ways than they can imagine. Not all people are wise enough to see the inter-connection. And to those who are, the world doesn't give them a chance. It is such a burdento know you are a would-be prophet and not be accepted by your potential *chelas.* Anyway, I am a brave kid. At least I was. I could bear with others' incompetence calmly. But I couldn't withstand the stubborn rigidity of Sushant anymore.

"If not for you I would have entered the cage and caught the lion. But you na, I tell you!"

Fulli served tea now. Sushant blew into it.

"You always do like this. Discourage me even for IIMs. You never include me in your discussions around it. As if…as if…"

Then Sushant said something which I needed to hear to run after it. He told me that I cannot do it. "You sound like a bloody *dehati*. And you don't even know who Julia Roberts is." Once I came to know I declared that she just cannot do a nude scene. "It is like Madhuri Dixit going nude. Impossible. What respect will she be left with?" I had roared. He arranged for a CD of a movie with dearest Julia's nude scene. Didn't I say he was an angel? It looked like that at that time. Bastard. He was actually a demon. I don't believe in them. But they exist. I have been running behind this thing called CAT ever since. It has coloured both, my real and virtual world. Would cram words from the dictionary. Words I knew I didn't know. Words I didn't know existed. Words which might as well not have existed. Words which I would struggle to find use of. Words my friends would struggle to find meaning and utility of, as I had completely given up on my mother. Oh, mother tongue I mean. Slip of tongue. Just a matter of tongue here and there you see. My friends had to bear with it. My usage of English and ghusedofying words of the day in our conversations. Others too tolerated with amusement at times. What choice did they have anyway. *My companionship came at a price now. One had to tolerate me.* When they refused to, I turned to the virtual world. Logging into yahoo chat room and saying random things to random people. It didn't matter what they were saying. What I cared for was what word I wanted to practice that day. Would talk to the mirror. Repeat the day's conversations in English at the end of the day. I had even begun to have dreams in English. Sometimes I didn't understand my own dreams because of language problem. Others in my dream didn't know my words and I theirs. Didn't know their words I mean. All this jumbling up hadn't got me anywhere. *Been seven long years! Huh! What a waste of time. So much so that I don't even get dreams anymore. Neither in English nor in Hindi. Who but a demon will do that to you, I ask. I could have run behind better things. Garima I mean.* No? Romantic musings? Escape mechanisms? I know. I know. Truth is I do not like rejections. No one does. I do not like failures. No one does. That's why I keep getting them all the time. Rejections I mean. Probably God wants me to fall in love with them. This is one of God's omens that I have not been able to accept. I hope he changes its meaning soon. Else, I will have to change him. God, I mean. That's not possible you say. I know. I know. That's why I am so depressed. Not good enough a reason to be depressed you say? Won't say, I know, I know. For I know that you are wrong. But would not tell you what is correct. For you don't care. And it's useless to talk to people who don't. Care I mean. Such a hopeless world it is. To hell with the 'word', sorry 'world' I mean. Slip of tongue. Just a bit here and there, you see. Let me take you back. Memories are not very pleasant here anymore.

3
THE FORTUNE COOKIE

Sorry, I completely forgot about her. Garima I mean. If you are thinking there are way too many of them, 'I mean' I mean, just wait a little. You will get used to them. Anyway, forget it. I had met her, Garima I mean, just a few weeks ago, rather heard her, over phone as she tried selling credit-card of the bank she worked with. I had recently been rejected in love and dejected at work. I always have been. Rejected and dejected I mean. I really have been. After a couple of years of high-speed performance and top level appreciation, suddenly the fortunes had changed. I had been moved to an assignment which had a reputation for spoiling careers of those who joined it. The client was prestigious, business was big, but the work was that of a donkey. And more importantly the person heading it was himself a donkey. The world is full of idiots. It really is. I don't need to tell you that. You can just look into the mirror, can't you? I know you can. Such a good old idiot you are. Anyway, back to myself. Used to having my way in my previous assignments, here I lost my way very quickly and would often get into arguments with the project head and sometimes with colleagues. By the time I realized that in the land of donkeys, horses are not desired, being a mule is good enough as long as you walk the line; it was a bit late. Ratings were down, relationships got spoiled and work piled up. First I fought, then I resented, and then I caved in. In short, I was depressed. It didn't help that I was in love with a girl with whom I knew I had a very little chance. Being in love with her was almost like watching a porn movie. You want to be in the movie yourself with the girl in there and you feel almost as happy as the guy in reality with her till the time the movie is on. But once everything is over and reality dawns, you feel shit and don't know whom to curse, your desire for her or the reality. This green eyed beauty was no *Aishwarya Rai* but to the besotted, that is me, she was no less. When I had first met her during a trekking group outing of our company, I had no idea that she would be able to cast such an effect on me. In a way I didn't even like her in the first go, there was no love at first sight, not even at tenth sight though she was still a sight full. I want to tell you so much more about her but you know what? It hurts. And there is already enough of hurt in this story. So just know that my chase for her was over even before it started. And I didn't have an exciting work scene to submerge myself in. In short, I was in a dark alley of sorts. I am often there. In the dark alley I mean. I really am.

Entered luv-Guru, Sanno. He had had a similar fate as mine but always used to keep smiling, which was both intriguing and frustrating. I had never known him to be a superstar of any kind, but what the hell, everyone has an ego. "How the hell can you take it all so lightly," I asked.

"Simple. Try Osho."

"Osho!!!"

"Yeah, Osho. Osho talks about *dhyaan*. That is what I do."

"You do *dhyaan*!!!" He was beginning to sound crazy.

"Yeah, but of a different kind. *Dhyaan* about my girlfriend," he winked.

"You have a girlfriend? How come I never saw you with her?"

"Yes. Remember Pinky?"

"Pinky? That daughter of your landlord???"

"Yes."

A wicked smile was floating all across his face while my head swooned with disbelief. Sanno's landlady treated him like her son. Her college going daughter, Pinky, would come up to him with maths queries.

"So...so, that is what you do with her in the name of solving maths questions?" I was almost screaming. "I never expected you to be so...so...smart. I always thought you were mild and simple."

Sanno gave me one of those smiles of his which I earlier took for simplicity and at times for stupidity but now I almost saw Osho's face in his.

Taking Sanno's advice to heart I began to hit on every girl I could. I tried all routes, dating websites, office colleagues, and references from friends with successful track records. There were some false starts too, but nothing that lasted for long. I was having an adventure but fun was all Sanno's. Once I came back completely frustrated and dejected from a blind date, and landed at Sanno's place.

"What happened? How did it go?"

"What happened? Can you not see it in my face? It was fucked. I was fucked."

"Why, what happened?"

"She was not beautiful, not even good. She was quite ugly and since I didn't want to hurt her as you had once said, 'Make a graceful exit if you don't like someone', I had to spend full five hours with her, go around the city tour in her car while wanting to run every second of it."

"Hahahahaha...you are such an idiot. *Arre*, it was just a few hours, how does it matter. She has a car so you don't even need to spend money on her. Keep her till you find the next one."

I gave Sanno a stare. "May be it does not matter to you but it does to me. I can't pretend and can't be somewhere once my heart is not into it. And I hate to make someone feel bad as well."

"Boss, you will not take the bad ones, and would never get the good ones. In short, nothing can happen with you."

"What?"

"Just have patience and some cool. It will happen."

"God knows. It better happen fast. I am losing nerve. Today again I had a fight with Mr. Donkey at office. This guy irks me. He seriously is an idiot yaar. He hates new ideas, in fact any kind of ideas unless they are his and are stupid."

"And your problem is you like only your ideas. Now relax and let's go out for dinner."

I had no other option but to do as he said. He was my luv-Guru after all, even if he hadn't been successful so far. And a ride on his bike always made me forget the day's disappointments. As usual, Sanno was right. I landed up with Garima within a few days. And Maya too. Did I mention her earlier? Oh, forgot to. Will tell you about her in a bit. Let's finish Garima first. I mean finish her story.

"*Arre*, don't call me please. I don't want it and I cannot give my friend's number," I heard Sachin request politely over phone. Sachin was one of the most dedicated and hardworking guys I had seen. His focus was less on work and more on hard.

"What happened Sachin?"

"Nothing *yaar*. This girl is repeatedly calling to sell credit card. She is asking for others' contact numbers also."

"Okay, do one thing. This time when she calls up, give her my number. I will handle her."

Sachin looked bewildered. "Trust me. Give my number to her. I can handle this."

Soon she was calling me.

"Hi, I got your number from your friend..."

"Sachin. I know. Tell me what have you got to offer?"

"Sir, our bank has launched a new credit card which has lots of benefits..."

"I know all that. Every bank offers these. What is so special about your credit card? Why should I take yours?"

"Sir, I have a target to complete. Won't you help me with this? And why are you talking so rudely while all other guys of your company talk so politely. I am asking you for help like a friend."

"Friend!! Then you should talk like a friend. Then I may think about it."

"But, that is how I am talking. Am I not sweet to you?"

"Yeah, but that is because you want to sell your credit card. You would not call me ever once I have signed up for it, will you?"

"No, nothing like that. I will."

"Okay, then call me after office hours and I will believe you. And if I take your card, a few others of my friends will take it as well."

"Okay, I will."

I hung up the phone and shouted to Sachin, "She will never bother us again."

She surprised me by calling after office hours. After some casual chat, I had no option but to acquiesce to her request.

"Okay, I will take your credit card and will also get you a few of my friends' contact numbers."

"Thanks. You are so sweet."

"It's fine. You are welcome." "Don't forget to send an e-card like you promised," I said as an afterthought. Just one call was not good enough for making such an effort for a girl. "You are just too soft," I heard Sanno say in my head.

"Sure, talk to you tomorrow. Bye."

"Bye."

Over the next few days I worked as an unpaid employee of the credit card company, convincing friends to fill up forms. I was yet to fill up my form though as I wanted a photo card and couldn't get my photograph clicked.

"Do you really want to take our card or you are just making a fool of me," she asked during our third after-office talks.

"No, no. I will, just that my photograph is not there."

"I don't believe you."

"Okay, if I do not take your card, then I will take you out for a movie. Okay?"

"No...no. You take the card then I would come for the movie," She said after a pause.

"Oh, ok. I will fill it up by tomorrow then," I said sheepishly, bit surprised by this sudden twist. I wasn't sure if she would come for the movie but the banter was good.

"I had thought that this guy is playing really smart. He is saying that he won't take my card and will date me as well. So I said take it and then I would come," she told me that Sunday as we watched the movie. This blind date didn't make me want to go blind.

They say if you keep your fist closed, you will squeeze everything you have out of it. Open your palms and everything in the world is yours. Something similar was about to happen to me. I was still to open my palms. I told you about angels and how I believe in them. I was about to meet a second one.

Her name was Bhairavi, my team member, and an odd ball friend for being a complete contrast. She was talented, erudite, and polite. And a lot humble. I was capable of being a loud mouth, hardly read, and could get aggressive. We met on a trekking trip wherein I had got besotted with a green eyed beauty. I hardly noticed Bhairavi there. I was busy trying to get the green eyed X-ray turn towards me by acting funny. Sometimes being an outright buffoon. She was hardly impressed. Barely amused. They say God closes a door and opens a window. He did but I had no interest in the window. You can't get a bed in from a window, can you? Unless it is a folding bed or you get wood in pieces and then assemble them inside. But what about the cost? And the effort? But God doesn't think of all this, I tell you. He can be such an impractical moron at times. Or at least the people he makes write these phrases about him. Anyway, he is accountable for all that goes around in this world. If he cannot take responsibility for all that goes wrong in my life and yours and everyone else's, he must for all the misleading phrases he comes up with. Such a nuisance they are I tell you. Anyway, the thing is Bhairavi got mighty interested in me. Not as a boyfriend-girlfriend thing but as a friend-friend thing. "You are so funny," she would keep on saying. Not so much in words but in that smile that she kept throwing at my every crass joke. To get her off my back, I tried to make her at the receiving end of my joke. "Bhairavi, it is impossible to talk to you. It is almost like talking to someone sitting on a passenger train while sitting in the Shatabdi. By the time you open your mouth to say something I am thinking of the answer to your response to the comment that I am about to make." I hoped that she would balk and tell me what an insensitive creep I am and would just keep her face away from me all the time and tell every other girl she meets, "I believe in morons. I know one." But no such luck.

One day I told her I had a gift for her and asked her to close her eyes and open her palms. She did. Such a trusting person she was. I placed a hair on her palm and stood there smiling mischievously. She shrieked as she opened her eyes. My job was done. Off my back she was. But not for long. She became even nicer and would laugh off my irritation. What you can't resist, you shall give in. I did the same. I became friends with her. Soon I knew why. When I was undergoing mild depression I told you earlier about, I was fervently looking for something to hang on to. Something, some succor, some idiotic line, something, even if stupid, that will make me believe in the moments to come. One day as I walked into Bhairavi's cubicle, I found it. It was written on her idea board. It said,

If you can meet with triumph and disaster
And treat those two imposters just the same;
Yours is the Earth and everything that's in it,
And which is more you'll be a Man my son!

Like I said, when you open your palms, everything flows towards you. When you don't have a question, everything looks like a solution. Suddenly everything looked like an opportunity. I wanted to be a man. Not that I had any doubt about my being one. I mean, you know what I mean. Yeah, that's what. I stopped sulking and drew out a plan. *I want a new girl and a new job.* Sanno was helping with the girl part already. I needed to do something about this job thing. *I would come to office, work hard for the five days and entertain myself by fighting with Mr Donkey on everything we do not agree on. Some satisfaction I must get out of work besides the salary. On weekends I would just go on job hunt.* But it would have been painful to do it alone. I decided to get Bhairavi in. She agreed. For a job or my company, I don't know. Didn't matter really. I was thankful that someone still liked my company. On weekends, we would search for job interviews in the newspaper and select ones we would appear in. It didn't matter if the requirement matched our skill or not. Idea was to go for the interviews irrespective of the outcome. It was like a game to us. She had a scooty, which we would drive around the city.

Slowly I began to see her like a boy should see a girl. She was prettier than I had thought. She wasn't too conscious of it though. Like a girl should be. Or like I wanted a girl to be. But what the hell. How good was I with that? She was smart, talented, and could stay put with me. Isn't that a great deal in itself? I suddenly wondered why she goes around with me for interviews. *She certainly doesn't need a job switch, though she would like to, as desperately as I want. She isn't that aggressive, nor restless.* She was doing it for the fun of being with me, may be. Just to keep me company may be. After the lunch they served a fortune cookie. I opened it. 'Wait before you make any decision about your feelings,' it said. I decided to. I believe in these stupid things. I do. I am rather stupid too. *One day I will bring her here again and propose to her. Would ask the waiter to serve a fortune cookie with message written from me. 'I love you,' it would say. Would be so romantic!* I imagined her reading it and smiling. I began to smile too. She found me looking at her with that lost smile. She waved her hand.

"Where are you? What are you thinking?"

"Oh, nothing. Just like that. Let's go."

Life went on.

There is a button somewhere in my mind. This button has a special feature. Once it gets switched on, I cannot stop. The way to switch it on is to tell me that I cannot do something. A new bunch of people had joined our project team. Sanno and I, stood like senior folks near the staircase assessing the new joinees. And then she walked past. Maya. She had grace. She was pretty. She walked in awareness of it. I was unaware of her effect on me. I gawked.

"Forget it," Sanno said.

"What?"

"Forget her."

"What do you mean?"

"Way ahead of us. Out of league."

"Yeah. I agree," added Nirmal. Another of starry, sorry, stare-eyed.

Who decides what my league is? Nobody. Who decides what I can do or not do? Nobody. Not even myself. Not even my own fearful small self who is afraid of failure and rejection. I go for the gold.

I began to plot a way to reach up to her. It was a tad difficult. She had a totally different set of friends. She was totally different from me. But isn't everyone totally different from me? Yes, everyone is.

There was something about her which used to bring out something different out of me. When I watched her from a distance I would lose all awareness of myself. A half smile would always be planted on her face like the freshness of morning dew. She would smile at some of my antics, at my efforts to grab her attention, making me shy and recluse. I would be laughing for no reason for the rest of the day. I soon figured out that there was no easy way to reach her. She was a part of my project team but the team was too big. She worked with a totally different set of people and sat at the other corner of the floor. She mostly kept to herself and it looked as if, she came, worked, and then left for home. The only time I could catch her was at the end of office hours while we waited for the elevator but then she would rather take the stairs. Huh! If not, then there would be a hell lot of people waiting outside and I would be lost in the crowd. Strange are motivations of people, at least mine. I began to try other routes to get her attention. Friends began to wonder about my sudden change of behaviour. I had become too vocal in project meetings and project gatherings. Normally I would talk about work only when I would work. That is, just work and forget about it. Now I spoke about anything and everything at any time, all the time that is. They were puzzled with my sudden crusadership. But the average software coolie could never gauge the meter of those who want to fly high, airport coolies I mean.

"It would not work *yaar*. All this doesn't work," Nirmal threw his judgement along with several grimaces at Sanno and me during one of our regular coffee breaks. I thrust my mouth into coffee dreading that he knew my secret. If he told others what I was after, I would have become a joke. I liked to crack jokes, not become one. Nirmal was from *Bihar*, wore a moustache, and was rooted in his behaviour and mindset. He may not have approved of office romance at all.

"What?" I whispered.

"You don't understand Romal. You are too naïve even though you yourself are from Uttar Pradesh."

"What do you mean?" I was a bit confused.

"*Arre*...that donkey promotes only people of his caste. I don't know how come you don't understand this. Even though it is an MNC, it runs all around caste politics."

"Oh, that...yeah...maybe..."

"Not maybe. Look at what had happened in the last six months. All the guys who got promoted were either from his state, his caste or his college.'

"Yeah, you are right. But there is no harm in trying. If I still don't get promoted, well, tough luck."

"Okay. As you wish," he said and left the two of us.

"Try the friend route," Sanno said softly as he always did.

"What?" I reacted as I always used to.

"I mean try reaching upto her through her friends."

Bastard knew what I was trying to do. "But I hardly know any of her friends."

"So know them. Make them friends first."

"How?"

"It is not me who is after her. If you can't make her friends your friends, then forget her."

His statement hit me like a bullet. I looked in her direction. Couldn't see her from behind her cubicle wall but could clearly see the guy sitting opposite to her. Narayan. My target. My prey.

Narayan proved to be an easy target. I hung myself down his cubicle wall like a roach wondering on the programming code he was writing.

"How very interesting and cutting edge this is! CAD/CAM, is it? And here I am wasting my life with eons old Java! Silly me." Mock laugh. Wave to someone from the other side of the floor. Quick disappearance.

Such short visits were becoming very frequent. Post my verbal duels with Mr Donkey in project meetings I would stick to Narayan, ask his feedback on my queries and drop him to his cubicle. Quick disappearance was the key to guerrilla warfare. Never let the target get too engaged to figure out that you are really short of ammunition.

Having established my presence, the next step was to encroach upon the territory and "put up my hoarding" there. This was accomplished by coincidentally appearing on the way to canteen while Narayan and company were on their way there. They used to leave around 4 pm for canteen. A few minutes before that I would leave my desk, reach downstairs, hide myself and come out once they had walked past and would meet them on the way to cafeteria. For these daily meetings, I had to dig deep into my reservoir of stock expressions for pleasant surprise mixed with hassle due to disruption in my deep thoughts that I was otherwise lost in. Over the diet of *paper dosa*, the *masala* for our love story was being prepared. Soon I began to feel that it was time to check its taste before I begin to sell it to the market.

There was no further need for meeting them on the way as I had now become a regular member of the group and it was okay to hang down other corners of Narayan's cubicle. On one of these days I expressed my unwillingness to be able to come for a plain dosa diet due to an overload of spice in my work.

"Would have to stay back and finish work. May go for lunch around 05:30 pm in case you people can wait. Leave it. Go. Would find someone later," is what my mail to them said around 03:30 pm. After a couple of responses, came the one I was waiting and hoping for.

"Let us all go later. I also am not feeling hungry enough at the moment," Maya.

"But I am very hungry. Why don't Romal and you go later?" Narayan. I didn't know whom I loved more.

"Okay," Maya.

"Okay," Romal.

Branch office had been opened.

4
THE PREY

I sat with her on the couch. Room was resonating with discomfort. She was visiting my apartment for the second time and that as per luv-Guru was a signal to become adventurous. I was good at getting girls up to the couch but poor at proceeding further. Till it was about chasing, it looked fun and fine. Try tricks, get beaten, get embarrassed, and laugh it off with friends. No one is getting hurt, right? But the problem surfaced once things went beyond fun. The big question would come up. Do I really like her? It had been a nemesis of my crossing the boundary line of being a boy. Today I hoped something would happen. I liked her company and she was transmitting the right signals.

"Have you heard about that line, Love once, marriage once but blah blah…?"

"No."

"Don't act innocent, of course you have. All boys know it."

I wanted to tell her that I am not sure yet of being a boy but am sure of not having heard this line.

"No, I really haven't. What is it?"

She gave me a dirty look. "Love once, marriage once, sex again and again."

I blushed. My heart jumped. The big day had come. Finally a girl with whom my conscience should not trouble me with the stupid question, *do you really like her*?

It is she who wants it, not me, I reasoned. I didn't get a go ahead but there was a soft silence, which I took for yes.

Switching on the television she surfed the channels before stopping at Fashion-TV. "This is what you like to watch, isn't it?"

I was aware of her overtones but was hesitant to take the first step. Somewhere within me, I felt a lock. As if part of me didn't want to go ahead. As if something from within was resisting my actions. *It is a headache enough to live with parts of me I can see. If I begin to listen to the locked parts of myself, life would be a nightmare. If he is not willing to open itself up, why should I worry what is it holding within.*

Coming close I hugged her and felt her face with my hand hoping that she would respond with clearer indications. She kept smiling and changed the channel instead. Remix of the song, '*Meri soni, meri tamanna*' was playing, catching her attention.

"What do you see in her? She has such a flat face and chest."

'Enough Romal. You can't be more of a loser,' I told myself. I held her hands with a resolve to kiss her but the ringing doorbell thwarted my attempt. She appeared bemused rather than perturbed at being interrupted. Irritated, I got up and opened the door. Saurabh was lurking, carrying his stupid grin, irritating me further. He knew I was with Garima and wanted to have fun at my expense.

"Do you have some milk, I am making tea."

I couldn't help grinning, said aloud "No," and began to close the door. He pressed the bell again. It left me with more grinning and more irritation. I went out, held Saurabh by the collar and dragged him away.

"*Abbe*, what is this. I just want to have a look."

"*Saale*, you just do *kaltofy*. It's not the right time."

"And what about the contract we had?"

Saurabh and I had a contract with each other sometime back that whenever there would be a conflict between a girl and friendship, friendship would be our priority. Saurabh was my colleague and lived in the flat above.

"See, this is not the right moment for that. Our friendship is still above her, but you are misusing it and also being indecent," I protested and tried returning to my apartment. Saurabh holding me from behind laughed uncontrollably at my urgency and embarrassment.

Coming back, I found her standing in the middle of the room, holding her bag, ready to go.

"I should be moving. Need to reach by nine else dad would get angry."

I cursed Saurabh for the mistimed entry and myself for the delayed efforts. I had planned a few more things. "Let us go inside, I have something for you."

In the bedroom I made her stand in the middle of the room.

"What?" She looked with her roving eyes trying to guess my intentions. Going by my performance in the hall, she didn't expect much.

I switched on the fan and rose petals began to fall all around her. I had placed them on the fan blades earlier wanting to create the Bollywood scene of heroine dancing in the middle of falling rose petals. "Would be quite dramatic and should impress her. Don't you think?" I had asked Saurabh as he grinned end to end and gulped his beer. He didn't want to lower my enthusiasm and wondered at my naivety. He could never make out how to react at my filmy ideas. He liked me but I gave him enough reasons to question our friendship.

Like hell I cared for what he thought as it got me what I had intended. Garima, impressed with my effort sealed my lips with a kiss. It may not have been the classiest idea but it had earnestness. I lost sense of time. But it came back. Time I mean. I was thinking about narrating my feat to luv-Guru and Saurabh, and about words of praise they would bestow. I was happier about my idea having worked rather than having been able to woo her. I pushed her back as she tried to get close again. *May be it's not the best time to go further. It's such a romantic scene, let me keep it this way else she would think I am desperate. This way I can win her trust and reap benefits for a longer time*, I reasoned. "I have something more for you," I said. I had brought two cross-necklaces from my last trip to Goa. I gifted one to her.

"Put it around me," she blushed.

She had forgotten about her timeline of nine. I decided to remind her.

"Let's go back else your dad would get real angry."

"Yeah, oh, yes. Okay," she said. *Stupid*, she thought.

5
THE OTHERS

Talk of Angels: Somewhere in the Sky

Trainee Angel: "This guy down there seems to be having fun. Strangely, I do not like it. Do you think I am jealous? Are angels allowed to be jealous?" He took a bow with his knees on the ground.

Mentor Angel: "Yeah, it is alright. You are new. It will take a few years before you disconnect yourself completely from human follies." He kept his eyes closed.

Trainee Angel: "But can I act on such feelings. Like can I really do something to…umm…steal his fun?" A slight embarrassment was evident in his tone.

Mentor Angel: "No, you are an angel. You are supposed to help people, not spoil their fun." His voice was stern.

Trainee Angel: "Yes, yes. You are right. Sorry for the suggestion." He began to back off. "But what about the girl? Don't you think he is taking advantage of her? Should we not do something about her?" A smile came over his face.

Opening his eyes, The mentor angel looked at the trainee angel. *He has potential. He is smart and can see a situation from multiple perspectives and choose the one favouring his desires. He is ready for grooming.*

Mentor Angel: "You have raised a valid point. Well done. We should do something."

Trainee Angel: "But we cannot do anything, isn't it? Because we are angels!!! Hah!!!" A tinge of disappointment mixed with envy was apparent in his voice.

Mentor Angel: "Well, you still have a lot to learn. We are angels. We are not supposed to curse anyone but we can surely give gifts to those we do not like…"

The trainee angel was confused and irritated. He didn't want to be an angel anymore. He never knew that angels have to give gifts to the ones they don't even like. If only he had known this before he had signed the term-sheet. He was contract bound for the next few years. "Hell. Now I know what hell is," he said to himself.

Mentor Angel: "…but you can choose the gift you want to give. Give him a gift that he cannot handle." A wicked smile came to him.

A feeling of reverence took over the trainee angel. He fell on the feet of his mentor. What an idea! Give him a gift that he cannot handle!!! How come he didn't think of it?

Trainee Angel: "And what could be this gift, Sir."

Mentor Angel: "Easy. Look into his head. See what is it that he fancies but doesn't really know what he will do with it. He doesn't really understand it. Is not ready for it."

The trainee angel sat in meditation, peeping into Romal's mind. Romal's mind reverberated with a three letter word, CAT.

Trainee Angel: "Sir, this guy seems to love cats. I find this word scattered all over his head. Strange, but should we just gift him hundred cats?"

The mentor angel broke into a loud hearty laugh much to the chagrin of the trainee angel. "Which part of the world were you from when human?"

Trainee Angel: "Poland."

Mentor Angel: "Oh, now I understand your ignorance. CAT is a very prestigious MBA entrance examination in India."

Trainee Angel: "Oh, but such obsession. I mean more than half of his brain is full of it. What is so great about it? Was Mahatma Gandhi from that institute?"

Mentor Angel: "Huh. I am yet to figure that out myself. But it sure is tough to crack. I couldn't in my time. In hindsight it was good that I couldn't. I had a better life without it. More money, more fun, and less tension. Anyway, I like this guy. Let us give him what he wants. He wants to crack CAT, he shall."

They got busy hatching a plan. Mentor angel approved it as a training project which he planned to personally supervise.

Driving back, I felt elated and couldn't wait to meet Saurabh and Sanno. She had rewarded me for my good behaviour before getting into her building and promised to invite me in when her father was not around. I called them up. Sanno was occupied, probably solving Pinky, sorry, solving her maths queries but Saurabh joined in. I kicked his ass a few times for his sudden need for milk earlier and filled him in with the details of today's rendezvous. His look changed from the stupid grin to surprise.

"Why are you doing it to yourself?"

"Doing what?"

"You know, all I can see is that your heart is not into it. You do not really want to do anything with her, you are just pretending, not to her but to yourself. Why are you doing it?"

"What are you talking about, dude? Of course I will do it, just waiting for the right time. You see, I have ample time. Haven't you heard about that story, never kill a hen who lays golden eggs?"

"Whatever. As long as you know what you are doing. Anyway, one more beer?"

"Sure. And don't worry about me. I know who I am."

I returned home late at night, slightly drunk after dropping Saurabh to the railway station as he had to catch *Goa Express* for his home, Delhi. Parking my bike I moved towards my flat when the watchman stopped me.

"Sir, you live in flat 103?"

"Yes, why?" I became aggressive expecting him to complain about something.

"Sir, there is a telegram for you. I was trying to find you the whole day."

"Oh. Yeah, I was working late today."

It was a small telegram and writing was not legible. I stepped back under the street light and read it aloud.

'You have been selected for *IIMT, Ghaziabad* and PI will take place on 3rd of March,'

It made me go numb. *I got a call from IIMT, Ghaziabad! When did I apply for it? Oh, admission for it was linked to CAT. Hell! My gut feeling of losing by a close margin was indeed true! Hell, what the hell. It validates without doubt that I am an idiot. If I had prepared a little or had more luck on my side, Rupali would have been telling my story to others instead of Puneet's. Hell, hell, bloody hell.* I wanted to smash something or bang my head into something. I hated half measures, I hated consolation prizes, I hated losing much more than I loved winning and I couldn't face it without any defense like it was then. The token success reeked more of failure by close margin than of any kind of success. Looking upwards I silently cursed. Little did I know that it was being well received.

It took a while for the feeling of dejection to melt.

Wait a minute. I never applied for IIMT, Ghaziabad. I had applied for MDI not IIMT.

But maybe you did. Do you remember it clearly?

Well, no, not sure. But I think so.

You think of a lot many things. That's your problem. Stop thinking and start accepting.

And its name was not IIMT but IMT.

Again, how much do you know. May be the name has changed for all you know. You never cared enough to read names of institutes properly. You had even forgotten to bring your mark sheet and other documents when you joined your company.

Yeah, yeah, yeah, yeah. But then no one had told me about it. It was my first job. I had no experience. There was no one to guide me.

Hah! It was there in your appointment letter. You never read it.

Yeah, but…

And, you had to travel back to Ayodhya to bring it back. And that too without a ticket, by train, sleeping on the floor.

Okay, I agree. You are right. Sometimes I can be a bit, well… careless.

Sometimes!!!

Come on, give me a break!!!

Okay, okay (smile).

Miffed, I picked up the telegram and jerked when I noticed something.

Hey, the stamp on it is from Indore. Isn't that strange? What does it mean?

Well, yeah. It is a bit strange. May be…ummm…this time CAT was managed by IIM, Indore that's why the letter is from Indore.

Umm…no…I remember very clearly it was managed by *IIM*, Ahmedabad this time.

Well, your memory again…

Well, shut up! I know this. Remember, there was this whole controversy around it?

Well, yeah. You do have a point here (Hate to give in).

And, if you look closely, may be this is not IIMT but IIMI instead, mark on T is not clear. Isn't it?

Well, yes. But what does it mean (concerned and involved in the mystery).

Can it, can it be that…that… (slightly excited)

Hey, wait. Let us not jump to anything (suppressing excitement). But what about that Ghaziabad thing. I agree it will be too much of a bad coincidence to have name of an institute changed, the letter coming from a different city without you having applied for it. You can be forgetful at times, but you are not that bad, I know.

Thanks buddy.

That's fine. But what about this Ghaziabad thing. This is plain confusing.

Let me read again. I read somewhere that we read with our notions, not what is written. And if reading comprehension marks are an indicator, then I do not read, I assume.

Hmmm…so why don't you read one letter at a time this time.

Okay. Here you go.

Y . . . O . . . U … Y o u … H … A … V … E … h a v e … B … E … E … N … b e e n … s e l e c t e d … for…I…I…M…T/I…G…D…and…P…I…will take place… hey…what the hell…hey…hey…hurray…it's not Ghaziabad… it's GD…Group discussion…it's not IIMT dude it's IIMI… hahahahahahaha….

Hahahahahahahaha…love you buddy… finally you did make me proud…

A little late and a little less but…

It's okay, little boy. Sorry for being strict at times but I wish you well. Always.

Yeah (tearful). Thanks for keeping a watch. What would I do without you?

Hey, I don't like no teary weary, you know that.

Yeah, neither do I. I am a tough guy.

Talk of Demons: Somewhere else in the sky

Trainee Demon: "I found out."

Mentor Demon: "What?"

Trainee Demon: "What keeps the two angels smiling?"

Mentor Demon: "What??"

Trainee Demon: "It is a trick they are playing with a boy. They gave him a gift he cannot handle."

Mentor Demon: "What!!!"

Trainee Demon: "Yes, bastards, smarty pants. Found a way to have our pleasure with their tricks. I have come to admire them."

Mentor Demon: "What????"

Trainee Demon: "Sorry but you got to give it to them. You know sir, I had a thought."

Mentor Demon: "What?"

Trainee Demon: "Why not join the party. Let us give him a curse too without telling the angels, will be kinda fun. Don't you think?"

Mentor Demon: "What!!! Hmmm…"

Trainee Demon: "What…what do you think of it…sir?"

Mentor Demon: "I am loving it."

6
THE RUSH HOUR

Time blurred. After the initial euphoria, I felt the need to share the news. I called up Saurabh. His train was still to leave.

"Dude, guess what, I got call from IIM, Indore." I was surprised at the flat tone of my voice, sans any drama. Guess when happiness is genuine, histrionics fall down.

"Is it? Good dude. Congratulations." I was more surprised at the flat answer of Saurabh. I expected fireworks. I expected him to jump around with excitement and shower me with compliments, like, "…bastard…how the hell did you do it? I never thought you can do so. You surprised me and I am happy for you man."

There was nothing like that, instead, there was a query, "…but did you appear for CAT?"

"Yeah, I had. I have been appearing for last four years. But after the failures of previous attempts, I stopped thinking and talking about it."

"And when did you prepare? I never saw you studying? Did you join any coaching institute?"

"No, I hadn't. Actually I didn't prepare this year. I applied because I did not want to have an excuse when the examination date approached, 'If only I had filled up the form, I would have prepared hard this year.' So I applied, no excuses, you know."

"Yeah, I know. Anyway dude, congratulations once again. And did you check for other institutes?"

"No, not yet."

"Why don't you do it? And keep me posted."

"Sure, will let you know if there is more good news."

I hung up, disappointed with Saurabh's matter-of-fact reaction. I had no one else to call up. It was 2 am and I did not expect much of a reaction from my family. *They would not have heard about the IIMs. They would be happy because I am happy not because they would understand the reason for my happiness.*

Taking Saurabh's advice I drove to an all night cyber-café. Being a regular visitor I directly took a seat. First I wanted to make sure that the telegram was true. *Who knows, whether it is for real or a mistake. It could be for some other Romal as well.* My apprehensions were baseless. I had indeed been selected for IIMI. Next, I checked for IIMA. *It is all or nothing, no half measures.* I couldn't help releasing a suppressed smile as the result came positive. It was too much of a surprise to react so I remained calm. I kept checking for other institutes, online results kept on saying the same thing, 'Congratulations. Your candidature has been selected...' They had never been so warm earlier. I went numb. Looking at the café owner, I thought if he had any inkling how my life has changed right here. I felt like getting up and giving him a kiss. Reading my intentions he hid behind his comp.

I walked out. Still in a daze, I called up Saurabh.

"Dude, guess what, I got calls from all the six IIMs," I said with a casual air.

There was a bit of silence. "What!! I never thought you were that smart."

"I know. Neither did I. But what to do? Luck is proving that I am. I am finding it hard to accept too."

"Hmmm…I really do not know what to say. Time to work hard buddy for the interviews. Have you done any preparation?"

I didn't know why Saurabh had started sounding like a big brother, but I played along. Interview and preparation for it was hardly there on my mental radar. I was too happy for the present to think about the future.

"I know. I will."

"Do you know why you want to do MBA in the first place? This is the first thing they ask you. Someone told me that IMS gives free interview preparation course to everyone with calls, you should go there."

Saurabh was taking all my joy away with his advice and tips. To cut him short I said, "*Achcha*, dude, I got to go now, I am sleepy. Will talk to you later."

"Sure. We will party hard once am back."

"Sure, bye." Breathing heavily I looked up. It was time to say thank you, but I didn't. It looked like too small a word.

What an interesting turn life had taken. Shaken me out of my sleep and left me with what? Excitement! There was lot to be done and little time to plan. There was hardly anything to plan. I called up IMS. They did have an interview preparation course for shortlisted students.

"What's the cost of it?" I enquired from the IMS counselor.

"What all calls you have?" Her tone was casual. I could picture her handling a few more people around her desk.

"All six," I said matter of factly.

"All six!" Her tone changed. She had probably stood up.

"Yes." I remained the same.

"Okay. Sir, why don't you come on Tuesday?"

"Sure. What time?"

"Umm...6 pm." Could sense that she has lost interest. That is as much time as anyone gives you. No matter who you are. Unless you give them time. I turned around. Bhairavi was sitting on her desk working diligently. My project team had absolved me of my duties. They would work without me as if I am among them. Allocate work to me then split it among themselves. Didn't I love them? More importantly, didn't they love me? 'What had I done to deserve this?' I wondered. I walked up to Bhairavi and shook her chair from behind. She turned towards me and smiled. Her messed up hair was spread across her face. Her specs had found their rightful place. Dark circles had begun to form below her eyes from the constant staring at the desktop and sincere work. But from out of it all, her eyes shone like something I didn't have a word for. They shone with purity. They shone with simplicity. I so very had begun to admire that. It is so reassuring, this thing called simplicity. Reassuring in its predictability. And that is what makes it boring.

"What's happening," she asked. A gentle smile on her face. Reassuring. Calming. Boring.

"Nothing." I turned to go. "You finish work. Will catch you later. Let's go to the canteen around 4," I added as an afterthought.

"Okay. Sure." She turned towards her computer. Without any thought in between. Simple. I had already turned towards someone else. Maya. Simple?

Maya was looking at her computer. Just like Bhairavi. Not with the same diligence may be. Who cares? I didn't. All I cared about was whether she cared. About me! Often I felt she was aware of her effect on me and secretly enjoyed it. That she smiles to herself after my orchestrated visits to her cubicle and mock chat with Narayan. But I wasn't interested in knowing if she did. What was I interested in? Good question. I stood at the corner of her cubicle. She moved her long, pretty, deft fingers on the keyboard. Wearing that crisp white dress she looked quite something. Her hair was left open and ended somewhere between her shoulders and her waist. A bit of wind would have strewn them into air. I visualized them flowing in the air like in *Yashraj* movies. It actually began to wave. She was waving her hand in front of my eyes. I felt the need to say something.

"What is that *Tikka* on your forehead?"

"It is ash from the *Ashram* in *Aurangabad* I visited last week."

"You go to an *Ashram*?" I had to say some more.

"Every year. With my family. My parents have been going there for years."

"Oh, Okay." Not much was left to be said.

"If you want I can bring it for you as well. It is auspicious." Her smile had widened. I was beginning to feel a few things which I couldn't understand.

"Yeah. Do bring it for me. It looks good. On you I mean," I mumbled.

"Now, let me work?"

"Yeah. I was just taking a break."

She turned back towards her computer. I began to turn as well. An image flashed in my mind. I saw us in the marriage mandap. I looked pretty delighted. She looked amused. I turned back and looked at her. The image was hers.

"Everything alright?"

"Yes...yes." I ran towards the washroom, splashed some water on my face and looked in the mirror. I looked just like I did in that image. I had lemon. I desired for guava and God had handed me mango. A bucketful of them. What was wrong with the world! The door opened and a girl walked in. She looked like Maya. I blushed. *I have begun to dream. But wait, I can see her reflection in the mirror.* She wasn't Maya. I was in the ladies washroom.

7
IT CAME THAT WENT

Life is unexpected. I don't need to tell you that. But I need to tell you something. Life looks the best when you are not even aware of it. Like I had become. You are really and truly happy when you don't need to tell anyone about it. They can see. You don't have any corner within you to see. It's all there. I rode on my bike. Today was the first day of the IMS interview preparation batch. It was also Valentine's day. Trying to be a good boyfriend, I asked Garima out. She refused. Her father doesn't allow was her excuse. Tried a couple more times. She still refused. I changed plans. I always do. Decided to go to IMS instead. Sanno wasn't pleased.

"You should try harder."

"But she doesn't want to go. Her father doesn't allow or something."

"That's just an excuse."

"Whatever. But she still doesn't want to go."

"She wants to see how hard you will try. Girls are like that. You don't understand it."

"Anyway *yaar*. Will handle her tomorrow. Let me go for the IMS thing."

"As you wish."

The traffic signal had turned red. Any other day I would have whizzed past. Today was different. I felt no need to be irreverent. I stopped my bike. A street child came and asked for money. Normally I would have refused. I was convinced that by giving money you only encourage begging. Today I didn't care much about myself. I didn't care about anything.

I slipped my hand into my pocket and took out whatever was there. Mobile, some loose papers but no money.

"Sorry, tough luck."

He looked on eagerly. Between us life was so unfair. I wasn't complaining. My mobile flashed. There were three missed calls. From Garima. *Shit! Why is she trying to reach me? Will call her once I reach IMS.* Signal had turned green. I reached IMS. Session had already started. Before I knew I was inside.

"How long is the session?" I asked someone.

"About two hours I suppose," someone answered.

It is six. That would make it eight. It's okay. She sleeps by eleven. I would call her after the session.

The session began. There was pin drop silence. Puneet was also there. The facilitator came. He never went anywhere. He called us to come forward and introduce ourselves for two minutes. No one stood up. No one wanted to be the first person. There was no need to. They were mules who move only for carrot. I am the donkey who keeps moving. I stood up. Puneet sniggered. *Hell with him.* I reached on the stage. Extempore began. Two minutes went by fast. So did five minutes. The pleasant smile on the facilitator's face was also gone. He tried to stop me. I was unstoppable.

"Just one more minute. It's very interesting story. The way I got my shortlist. So that evening..." I continued. I was overwhelmed by my sudden selection and deluged by events. Everyone listened to my tale. The facilitator had turned pale. It ended with a big applause. I deserved it. I didn't know if I was more pleased with the IIM calls or with its dramatic element.

"Now that is the perfect example of what not to do ever at an IIMA interview," the facilitator informed everyone. My smile remained intact but my heart shrunk. There were mock group discussions conducted afterwards. I was massacred. Partly because I find it difficult to speak in a fish market. Which is what it was. A fish market, I mean. Also the facilitator was avenging himself.

"Romal, your voice is too weak. Be a bit fast please," came down the facilitator. I tried. "Faster." I tried. "Harder." I quit. I decided to prepare on my own. These guys were breaking down my morale. Damn useless these guys are, I tell you.

I left IMS at quarter past ten. Tried calling Garima. She didn't pick up. I called again. She still didn't. I kept calling.

"Hello."

"Hello. Hi. Sorry, I couldn't take your call earlier. I was..."

"...with some other girl. Weren't you?"

"What?"

"Don't play innocent. I know you guys very well. You didn't take my call because you wanted to go out with someone else. Who is she?"

"What?"

"Shut up. You didn't even ask me to go out?"

"What?"

"Stop doing this what what thing. I was testing you. You failed."

"What?"

She disconnected. "Bee...bee," it said. I tried again. She had switched it off. And that was that. Some love stories are just not meant to be. Like all others. And it was never love to begin with. It was just play. If it was love, it would have hurt. If it would have hurt, I would have found a way around it. I stood holding my mobile in my hand for a while before I began walking towards my bike. Hands in pocket, head hung low. "I got her over a call and lost her over a call," I mused to myself. As I rode my bike, wind splashing against my face, my left foot swiftly changing gears, a smile returned. Hugging my body close to the bike, I sped up. It skidded suddenly and I began to fear losing control and hitting the road. I straightened up and brought it under control. I halted and stood on the side of the road to take a breather. "I need to keep a grip on myself and focus on the road ahead," I told myself as I rode it again. *And I need to let go of what is getting left behind and embrace what is to come.* I began to speed up again. This time with a little more caution. It was difficult to stop me. It was difficult to hold me. Only I could have. Handled myself I mean.

8
THE INTERVIEWS

IIM, Indore interview was the first. I couldn't make a plan for it. If you have a plan, great, else you still got to play. I hid my nervousness. My name was called out. A middle-aged professor with a large paunch and a countenance telling that smile never visits him, welcomed me and gestured to take seat.

"You are interested in Jewish history?" I had mentioned so in the form.

"Yes sir. And there is a very interesting reason behind how my fascination for it began."

He had no interest in my story. He threw a few questions about history which I answered with some mistakes. He seemed impressed, less by my knowledge but more by my unusual interest.

"Have you read *O' Jerusalem*, by *Dominique Lapierre*?"

"No, sir," I said realizing that it was something important.

"That's alright, you should sometime."

"Sure, sir." Smile found a place on my face as he seemed happy with me. I didn't realize that my frivolousness had also crept in.

"And what is this interest in journalism? You have indicated that as your alternative career choice."

"Yes, sir. I am very interested in it and seriously thinking about taking it up."

He probably expected a more reasonable answer but something in my face told him that he should rather not.

"Do you know where Nilgiri mountain is?"

"Ummm…somewhere in south sir, not sure."

"Atlas?"

"No idea, sir."

"Vindhyachal?"

"Ummm...don't know sir." I wondered if I looked any bit like a *Sherpa* because of which he was suddenly testing my knowledge about mountains. I couldn't see any connection of it with MBA education, till something hit me.

"Oh, now I know why you are asking me about the mountains. I was wondering so. It is because I have written my hobby as trekking, isn't it? Actually sir, I have just been to one trek so far and that too only near Mumbai. I am no serious trekker sir. I really do not know much about the mountains," I enlightened him as he grunted in gratitude which I responded with a wide grin. Thoughts about the green-eyed beauty returned at the mention of trekking. For a moment I felt like telling him my real reason of trekking.

"Okay. Let me see. You have said here that you also have interest in arts. What do you mean by that?"

"Art, sir. I mean general art. Drawing, painting, creative stuff," I blabbered. He gave me a long, hard look.

"What are the top awards in the area of arts?"

"Umm…I won't know sir."

"And you are interested in arts?"

I stayed silent. I suddenly remembered I had included these as my hobbies to test the kind of questions they will invite. I wanted to use this interview as a preparation for the rest. *What is a little embarrassment in the larger scheme of things? What does he know of my subtle plan? I am using you fat buddy.*

"Okay, Romal. Have you heard about Satpura ranges?"

I actually had heard about them. "Yes sir. I have. There was this poem in junior classes, 'Satpura ke Ghane Jungle'. Isn't it the same one?"

"Yes, the same," he said with a frown as he began to get impatient. "Can you tell which state it is in?"

I thought about reminding him that it is not really my hobby. But he already knew that. I wasn't too sure where it was. Just that it was somewhere in the central India. I tried my luck. "Sir, it used to be in Madhya Pradesh…" His eyes popped open at my statement wondering if I meant that mountains can also move across states. Even his thickset face began to have an expression, of shock.

"…it could be in Chhattisgarh now, after the division of state, I am not sure." His eyes took their normal position as he realized I maybe idiotic at times but am not an outright fool.

"Have you got calls from other IIMs too Romal?" he made the parting query. I took it as my last chance.

"Yes sir, I have. Actually I have it from all the six. I know it is little unexpected with my kind of percentile. I guess it is due to my work experience…" I wanted to say more. I wanted to tell him the whole wonderful story of that fateful night. I opened my mouth but he showed me the door. I was done. I didn't have a good feeling about it.

Going by my debut I had a long way to go. Not that I was gaining anything from the experience. The harder I tried, the worse it got. IIMK interview I didn't care about and the IIMC panel didn't care about me. But this was a different day and a different college. It was IIMA, far beyond my reach, maybe. What the hell, no one decides where my reach is. At least I would not decide that for myself. I decided to not try to get selected. I would let them discover me. To manage my nervousness and sagging confidence, I occupied myself in a conversation with a colleague also there for the interview. She was looking over my shoulder. I turned back only to find someone calling my name, apparently for the interview. The person led me to a small room and took seat next to two other panelists and started with a barb, "Here is a guy more interested in knowing answers outside than facing questions inside". I ducked it, responded with a gummy smile and took seat. The other professor, who looked the grim kind, perused through my form and added to the barb, "Engineering in Paints Technology and working for Information Technology! Interesting."

"You see sir, both have technology in them", the first one added with glee, "Isn't it Romal?"

I decided to duck it as well and kept smiling leaving them to wonder what's inside my head, not that there was much.

"Romal, you work with computers, tell me how many pixels are there in a computer?" the grim one asked. The first one kept smiling while the lady in the middle maintained a crestfallen expression.

"I don't know, sir."

Frown. "Okay, can you tell me how many colours can a computer display?"

Thinking. "I am not sure sir but what I have studied is that there are three basic colors and all other colors are formed by combination…"

"…Romal, don't try to take us around. If you know the answer, say so, else say you don't."

"I don't know sir."

"It seems you haven't been using your B. Tech. knowledge in your job, hmm?" A stare came my way.

"I was doing what they hired me for." I return their barb.

"You did your B. Tech. from HBTI, isn't it?" asked the first one.

"Yes, sir."

"Why don't you tell us more about it?"

I started with standard stuff which I had mugged having anticipated this question. The institute's full name was Harcourt Butler Technological Institute, with Sir Harcourt Butler being the Governor of Uttar Pradesh at the time of opening of institute.

"Hmm…was *Harcourt Butler* alive or dead at the time of opening of the institute? I mean was it named after him posthumously?"

"I believe he was alive at that time."

"You believe! You are not sure?"

"No, sir, I am sure. I think he was alive at that time."

"Still, you think! Romal, we want confident guys in here. Someone who talks with full confidence." Their voice had found strength and aggression. I decided to give it back. They wanted to discover me, let them find it.

"Sir, whatever I know about the institute and its antecedents, is mostly through the pamphlet they gave me when I joined. Now, what was mentioned in it is that, he was Governor of Uttar Pradesh at that time, what was not mentioned is whether he was alive or dead at that time. Now, I am a logical person and I am not aware of any British policy or any such policy anywhere in the world which allows dead people to be Governor of any state, thus logically speaking he must be alive at that time. I believe in what I think that is why I initially said, I believe followed by I think. And if you are still not sure of my confidence then let's place a bet and find it out, I would put my money on him being alive."

"Hmmm…Romal, are you sure he was the governor of Uttar Pradesh?"

Getting carried away with my own smartness I continued in the same vein, "Of course, again by the same logic. I do not remember reading the name of the place of which he was the governor but I do not remember any Governor of India with that name so logically speaking he must be governor of…"

"Yeah, yeah, we know, you believe in logic and think and believe in it."

"Yes, sir, you have got it right." I beamed as something filled me from inside. They absorbed the heat in my monologue with a studied silence, deciding to cool it off.

"Ok. Why did you choose to go to IT after doing your graduation in paints technology?"

"Sir, when I took paints technology, I just wanted to secure my bottom line. I wasn't really sure of how good or bad I was as I was the only one in my family or school to have got selected in an engineering college and I had never really seen myself as a great student or something. And this branch I was told gets everyone at least three jobs each, if not more. That was incentive enough for me to pick it up."

"Then why switch to IT?"

"Once I joined, I realized my mistake. There was no one to compete against there. I could stay afloat with literally no study. I also realized that jobs in paints technology do not offer enough exposure. That is when I decided to seek a career in IT instead."

"But you could have always developed some product and may be sell it on your website or something. Why limit yourself to Indian market in this new age of technology?"

"Yeah, may be one can do that. But I believe it will require too much self belief which I don't think I had. Also, it's not as if paints is my passion or something. I opted it for a career of some sort. It did not matter where does it come from, paints or IT or something else. And the way you are saying, it's possible but it's a zero or one game, all or nothing. I don't think I wanted that, I wanted to ensure something as it was about survival."

The two men nodded a bit while the lady in the middle remained unfazed and wore her sullen expression.

"Okay, Romal, we buy your point. Let us test if you learned something during your engineering at all because as you said earlier you have not used it in your job at least. So, tell me what kind of paint is used in ships etc.?"

"They are called marine paints. They are made especially water resistant by adding zinc in them." My heart filled with pride at doing some justice to my degree.

"Hmm…and what kinds of colours are used in rural India?"

"Rural India?"

"Yes."

I struggled to find an answer as my pride began to slip. I tried taking the smart cut again. "Sir, actually we were never taught any marketing stuff during our engineering and since I never intended to take up a job in paints I never studied it myself, so I won't really know."

"Hmm…Romal, try to remember something. We think you have

exhausted your quota of I don't know answers."

They seemed to be enjoying the battle. They put me in a fix and I try and wriggle out. I took up the cudgels. "Sir, though I have not read about it but I do belong to rural area so by observation I can say that they like dull colors."

"What?"

"Yes, sir. And that is why I guess distemper sells so much in rural areas. Logic sir, sheer logic," I said smiling.

"Oh, we see. So what kind of colour is popular in urban India? I presume you have lived there as well."

I returned their smile and continued, "I have and I know what you are asking. There is a particular name for it but I can't remember it. The kind of colours they show in movies these days, isn't it?"

Their smile shrank before it turned into a frown. "But sir if someone asks me to name it then I would call them fluorescent colors."

A constant frown found place on their faces. I sat anxious that I may have gone a bit too far when something else struck me. There was no Uttar Pradesh before independence.

"Sir, just remembered something. That question about Sir Butler being Governor of Uttar Pradesh you asked? Actually it was not Uttar Pradesh then but United Province..."

"That's okay. That moment has passed now. Leave it there Romal."

Everyone struggled to find a question which will not get an answer they don't want to hear.

"Hmm...we see that you have mentioned history and religion as your hobby. That's interesting, how did you get into this?" asked the first one.

I loved such questions for they offered ample space for bluffing. "Actually sir, it all started a few years back when middle east crisis was reported regularly in newspapers, with frequent blasts. My ignorance about its genesis made me feel ashamed of myself. Being an engineer and working in an IT company, we are in a way kind of educated elite but surprisingly we know nothing outside our narrow world. My surprise turned into a shock when I realized that I was not alone, my friends were not only ignorant but also indifferent. I began to read about it over the internet and then one thing led to another and soon history was all over me. Then as if by providence something happened which made me realize its importance even further."

"What is that?" For the first time they seemed genuinely interested.

"Actually sir, it's a bit funny. I was reading history of Pakistan on some Pakistani website. They had portrayed their history as if Pakistan was never part of India, at least not under a Hindu king, may be for a brief period if at all."

"What do you mean?"

"You see sir, Pakistan and India were under the same kingdom during the time of Asoka, who became a Buddhist, during Mughal period who were Islamic and during Britishers, who were Christians. It not only contradicted my beliefs as an Indian but on a separate note, revealed their insecurity about their separate identity. Identity away from and independent of India."

"And?"

"I wrote so as a feedback to their website and that is when the unexpected happened. I got series of mails from their administrator having deep anti-India messages, especially about Kashmir. I responded to initial couple of mails but soon stopped becoming wary of any backlash. Who knows, maybe they can track me via mails. But it further fuelled my interest in history. I realized, I may not care for where we come from but obviously there are people who do and they touch our lives in more ways than we know."

"Interesting, pretty interesting Romal. So, why don't you tell us a bit of history? You are from Ayodhya, right?"

"Yes, sir."

"So Romal, tell us something about Ayodhya which we don't already know?"

I was pleased. I had consumed more than ten pages of history about Ayodhya from internet. I started my speech from around 1000 AD. I barely made a couple of statements before being interrupted.

"No, no, Romal, don't tell us all this. Tell us something which we don't already know." They could smell my discomfort. Glee had found its way up to them.

I skipped a few hundred years and started from somewhere around 1400 AD.

"Romal, again the same thing. Don't try to take us for a ride, if you know, well say so else just say you can't."

He was deriving raw pleasure from the duel. I suddenly saw the origin of it. He was someone from near the place I was from, had the rawness and enjoyed verbal duels. I picked it up.

"See sir, I don't know what you don't know. I can only tell you what I know. Either you tell me what you want to know or figure it out yourself."

Realizing that we are evenly poised he played the grace card and took a backseat. I began my lecture on Ayodhya's history but lost my grip as I narrated events around and after 1900 AD. It gave him a chance.

"Romal, it seems like your knowledge of events post 1900 AD is not that strong, strange, for that is what you should be more tuned into."

Assessing him for a while, I found my bomb in my head and finally hurled it, "Sir, as I said my hobby is history, and after 1900 it becomes current affairs."

The expression on their faces told me that I have won the battle. Whether that meant I have won the war as well was something I had to find out. But I was savouring this win. I was loving it.

With the two men having lost their ammunition, the lady decided to take up the mantle.

"So Romal, which all religions you have studied?"

"Ma'am, I have mainly read Judaism."

"Just *Judaism*? And you call religion as your hobby?"

This time I was ready with my gun and I decided to fire it immediately, "Ma'am, actually I thought that since you are asking the question, you must be knowing that knowing Judaism means knowing Judaism, Islam, and Christianity as the three are interconnected and part of the same tree. I am Hindu by birth so obviously I would know about it and being an Indian would have decent knowledge of Buddhism and Jainism. That leaves out sects or religions with limited presence like Shamaism and Baha'ism which I did not think shall be mentioned. So I just said I have studied Judaism but of course I have studied others as well."

Her sullen face became even more so as others also did not seem to appreciate this attack. They decided to remain courteous and asked a few questions around Judaism which I answered with profound confidence. Soon my time was up.

"Ok, Romal, I think that is it. You may go now."

I felt that the interview was not being left on a very positive note, not negative but not positive either, so I made my last effort.

"No, no, sir, it's okay. I am okay with more questions."

"It's not about you but about us. I think we have seen enough of you. You may go now."

Time for fun was over and I had to move. Stepping out I felt, am either completely in or definitely out. They wouldn't need more than a moment to decide my fate.

IIMB interview followed. I tried repeating the trick I had used at IIMA interview. Be a bit witty and sincere when you can afford it. When cornered, wriggle out by throwing something unpredictable. Use your street humour to your advantage. It backfired. They didn't seem to like me much nor did they care much for my knowledge of history. I wasn't bothered much. I was happy that interviews are over. I had to wait for the results.

9

AND IT HAPPENED...

Waiting for the results was proving to be mostly uneventful. I decided to give it a twist. I had always acted like an underdog, underplaying my chances of winning or achieving anything. *What if this time I played like a bulldog who is brimming over with confidence? It would be a good game. What's the harm anyway?* I resigned from my company even before the results were out as irrespective of the outcome I didn't want to be there anymore. *I would either go for an MBA if selected, else would join the other company I have got an offer from. I am safe. If I don't get through after my boasting, I would not be here to face the embarrassment.*

Bhairavi became my first target as we, Bhairavi, Puneet, and I went out for dinner.

"Romal, when are the results coming out?"

"In a week or two I suppose."

"Oh. You must be nervous, no?"

"What nervous? See I don't care for IIM Indore and Kozhikode. I am not gonna join there in any case. IIML people just can't reject me. I wa too good for them you know. I could see it in their face during interview. They were talking to me in Hindi, *yaar*. Can you believe it?"

"Romal, don't talk like that. It is not that easy. Aren't you afraid of failing?" she asked. Puneet looked blank and confused.

"What failing yaar. What is true is true. See, I don't think I am interested in anything other than IIMA and IIMB."

"What about C?"

"What about C? There is no chance they will pick me up. I had a fight with the professor in the interview."

"You had what?"

"A fight. Not really a fight just that I got a bit pissed off because he was cornering me so I said something, well rash."

"What did you say? Tell me?"

I gloated at the effect I was having on them. Bhairavi's eyes widened with anticipation. I saw a lot of admiration there. Puneet looked dull. *What a day. Finally!*

"Ah, okay. Not really an interesting story though." I did *nakhara* before continuing, "I am horrible in group discussions as I fumble when ten other people are trying to hog up space. So I was big time screwed in IIMC GD. During the interview there was this professor who was after me about my poor performance in GD."

"So?"

"So, well he got after me about why I want to do MBA."

"And, what did you say?"

"*Arre*, what is there to say? You want to do it because; well you want to do it. Or rather, how can you not do it when they send you interview calls? I mean I got calls so I went for the interview, that's it."

"You didn't say that to them, did you?"

"Well, no. I was trying to do the SMD thing in that interview."

"SMD?" Eyes had widened further.

"Sincere. Motivated. Driven." "Didn't I mention it earlier?" I added with a bit of swagger. She broke into a loud laugh. I was enjoying every bit of storytelling.

"Yeah, you know, earlier my mantra was CCF, but after the IIM calls I realized it has to change to SMD."

"Now what is CCF?"

"Cool. Casual. And Freaky." I said with a genuinely sheepish smile while she appeared bewildered.

"Anyway, I was trying to evade 'Why MBA' question by throwing crap of all kind, like, 'MBA will let me view an organization with a bird's eye-view, top management view' and how as a software engineer I can only see limited view of business and all that."

"Then?"

"Then *kya*? He just got after me, ripped me and asked to explain this bird thing further. I didn't have an answer. He cornered me by asking one single question and demanded a single line answer, no fluff."

"What was that?"

"He asked me, why would I leave my job to do MBA?"

"And, you said?"

"Because I cannot do both of them simultaneously."

Bhairavi's expression changed from amusement to amazement to apparently reverence while Puneet looked flabbergasted. I may have failed at IIMC interview but I knew I have won something out of it. An impactful story worth telling. Ah, it was awesome.

Soon the results began to pour in. It was mostly on expected lines. IIMC had shown the door. IIML had opened its. IIMB too had chosen to remain silent on me. IIMA had yet to reveal itself. I waited for it with so very a bated breath that at times I felt choked and suffocated.

It was out the next day. I had gone to Bhairavi's home to help her setup her new TV. She introduced me to her flatmate, Swati, a pretty and pleasantly plump Bengali girl. Bengalis are intellectual, so I had heard. And there is nothing more pleasurable than poking fun at an intellectual by beating their well structured arguments with street smart lines.

"Bhairavi told me that you got into IIML. Congratulations."

"Well, yes."

"Aren't you happy about it? I would have been over the moon."

"Well, it's not really an achievement. It had to happen. It happened."

"So, what is an achievement then?"

"Well, actually to be honest, I don't know. You see there was no element of surprise in these results." Bhairavi walked in with tea at that time.

"What? You have again begun to slight IIMs?"

"I am not slighting. I am just saying what I honestly feel. Didn't I say that IIMC will throw me out? They did. I am fair on both sides."

"Ya...ya. So what are you saying?"

"I am saying that the only result I have some interest in is IIMA. The interviewers should not take more than a second to decide upon my fate. It's either in or completely out. My guess is in. But well I would like to see it now."

"So you will be happy if you get into IIMA? Right."

"I guess so. But I am already so clear about it..." I was interrupted as my mobile rang. In that brief moment I wondered how would I really feel when the results do come out? *If I get selected, will I be as ecstatic as I have thought at times. Will I just jump over from my building or run on the street and hug everyone there. Will I? What will I do? What if I am not selected? Will it affect me?* There was no answer. I answered the call. It was Puneet's.

"Romal. Did you check your results?"

"Yeah. I made it to IIML. B and C threw me out."

"No. I mean IIMA."

"No. Is it out?" My voice dropped, nervousness came over me. I controlled myself as I had attracted attention of Bhairavi and her friend.

"Yes."

"Did you make it?"

"No." I fell silent. Puneet's voice hadn't lost its usual enthusiasm though I sensed a jingle missing. I may have been hallucinating like I always do. Seeing too much into others' emotions while remaining unsure of my own.

"That's okay. I didn't expect to get through. You haven't checked yours, have you? Of course not. You didn't even know it was out. Why don't you check?"

"Yes, I should." Bhairavi's was looking at me expectantly. *Show time.*

"Puneet, why don't you check it for me. Do you have access to internet?"

"Yes. But would you not want to check in privacy. I mean, you know." Puneet was concerned that if results are not positive it will be embarrassing for both of us. I didn't want to miss the high that I could create by showing the audacity of getting the results over phone through someone else. Confidence, anyone?

"Okay, give me a minute." Excitement began to build in me. I was optimistic. Bhairavi and her flatmate were even more expectant.

"Romal, *Saale, Kutte…*"

"*Kya hua be.*" I couldn't sound casual and calm anymore.

"*Abbe, bhediye, chhappar phar diya.* You have made it *be*, you have made it."

"What? Can you check once again?"

"Yes. Of course. Why not. *Abe*, it's right. You have made it."

Getting up from the bed I looked at the two. *Shouldn't I be doing something dramatic? Will fit the scene.* I picked up two pillows and threw on the ground. "I have made it," I proclaimed. In my heart it felt like nothing. A few shallow dim ripples. I wondered why.

I felt aloof. I began to walk out of Bhairavi's place.

"Where are you going? Our treat? You cannot slip away like this. You are an IIMA guy now."

She was gushing, filled with surprise and pleasure, appearing dazed. She was happy for me. She was surprised at the sudden events she had witnessed unfolding. She was probably bewildered to discover that someone as ordinary as I could also reach there. IIMA I mean. But I didn't feel any pull towards her reaction. No place or person came to mind. A desire to move away arose.

"No, I will go now."

"Yeah, yeah. You shall. Let us all go out."

"Noo. Some other time. I…I…just want to be alone I guess. I don't know," I mumbled. Even speaking looked like an effort.

Bhairavi couldn't understand my sudden need for reclusion. I had never been like this. Reclusive I mean. Not known to anyone at least.

"No. I will come with you." She picked up her handbag. I couldn't insist anymore.

"Do you want to call someone? Your parents may be," she suggested.

I wasn't ready for it. They would hardly understand what it means to me. Even I hadn't begun to understand it. The dream, the fantasy, the mirage that I had been chasing without any real reason had suddenly become true. Become true when I had lost all hope and desire of it. I didn't know how to make sense of it. I could sense something happening to me. I needed to make sense of it first. I needed to be alone.

Bhairavi came along to my flat. I was walking in a trance. Her constant glare making me uncomfortable. The admiration in her eyes was unnerving. I wasn't used to such admiration. Opening my flat I entered in. She followed suit. Mattress and the television reminded of that fateful night with Garima. I smirked at my own foolishness. 'Would reap benefits over a long period of time,' I had reasoned. This is of no use, this rationalization I say. Reason is a good adviser, bad guide and a poor friend. But it didn't last for long. Smirk I mean. No memory looked attractive enough.

"What is it? You are smiling. What at?" asked Bhairavi. I understood that her query is more to elicit a response. Any response. She was completely bedazzled. I had become an inscrutable God to her. You revere him but do not understand him. I didn't know what to do with her. I gave her an observant look. Standing there dressed in her traditional kurta with her untidy hair falling all over, she had a charm that I had never understood. She looked meek and timid but she had a certain strength that I knew but couldn't understand. Just as she couldn't understand me. We were strangers to each other in a way. Isn't everyone a stranger to me? I didn't want to delve into any of it. There was something else. What was that? I felt an impulse to kiss her. I wondered how she would react. I let go of it. The impulse I mean. The idea of kissing her didn't look exciting enough. What was happening to me? I mildly asked her to leave me alone. She wouldn't move. Her fuzzy smile made it difficult to push my way through. Soon she understood and left. Not before telling me that she is there if I need company or anything. I said yes and closed the door on her. I didn't want to be rude, not to her. But I had to be alone. I stood in the middle of the room. The fan was whizzing above and the almirah with a mirror stood in the front. I had used the same mirror to put a locket around Garima's neck. I pushed her out of my mind. I felt I was sinking into the unknown. I felt weird. I didn't want to. I liked to appear a bit weird to others, not actually being one to myself. I gave a few shouts to bring myself back. But I didn't come back. I decided to stop resisting and lay on the bed. A new set of memories began to play on my mind. Memories of Sushant and Khan. Of their speculating that I would drift away. Of Sushant scorning me that I cannot get into IIMs. And many other such memories of moments when I had felt small. When I had felt not the same as others. *So is it indeed true? The vague niggle I always have had that I am a little different from others? That I am bigger, larger, and probably smarter than others? That I am made to marry one of the three: Aishwarya, Sushmita and Sonali I mean.* I observed myself in the mirror. I must be the same as always but I felt I have become bigger, better and beautiful. My eyes had acquired a new shine. I couldn't stop looking into them. They had admiration for themselves. I was no more an ordinary boy. I opened up my shirt. Chest hairs had begun to sprung up. I caressed them with my finger. A lot of past was getting settled. A lot of future was getting planted. *I don't need to make sense of it. IIMA I mean. It would become sensible on its own. I just need to give things time. I just need to go along the wave. It will take me somewhere. Somewhere definitely better than anything I can think of.* I sensed something move inside me. Something lusty, someone wild had crawled under my ordinary skin and begun to show its fangs. His wild, hungry eyes were lurking from behind the ordinary me. A new me had begun to emerge. The ambitious me. The passionate me.

10

AND ALSO HAPPENED…

Getting selected for IIMA had left me disoriented. So far it was all a game, a could-be reality, it was fine. But after the initial song and dance it was time to actually enter the dragon. '*What am I supposed to do inside there!*' My mind wandered wildly. When looked at as an adventure trip with loads of events to come, it brought a smile. But often it looked like a responsibility, a noose, a need to make something out of the opportunity, suffocating me. I would quickly spit and clear my system of such notions. Saurabh would kick my ass at every opportunity, so pleasantly surprised was he. He claimed to everyone that he has contracted my posterior for next couple of months. I had begun to kind of like it. He didn't know but sometimes I would secretly hug him on the pretext of crushing him between my timid arms. Okay, they were not so sticky after my sojourn with the company gym in the last couple of years. He didn't know how badly I was going to miss him. I had begun to feel that already. *It is indeed a monster, a dragon that I am entering. It is taking me away from all the things I have come to love and gotten used to. I am to enter alone.* Sometimes it would make me a trifle sad. I would ask Maya to accompany me to the canteen at those times. There is nothing a few smiles from a PYT can't cheer you out of. She had become kinder to my requests now and would often herself ask me out. On the buttery slopes of IIM tag, everything comes easy. Her eyes constantly suggesting something and my mind forever lost somewhere else, looking at myself in the reflection in the glass behind her. I don't know what I God damn found there. I am not a piece of art you know. She pushed the plate of *poha* in front of me, "Eat," she said.

"No, don't feel like." I was lost in my own reflection.

"You want something else? Shake?"

"No. Nothing. Just don't feel like."

"Drama! Drama! Don't do so much drama else it will be too late for anything." Her smile was intact nor had her voice any undertone. But I felt it was foretelling me something. I began to eat. I wanted to keep its taste and her smell in my memory for long. While God had been kind of late, I couldn't forget that there is justice in his domain. A little late it may be. *There are bound to be some disappointments coming my way. If they don't come soon, they will come as disasters later. Justice delivered late is served with accrued interest and penalty up there.* I wondered what that could be.

She got up to pay. I remained seated. There was nothing between me and my reflection now. We talked directly. I felt some tears. Okay, just a little moisture for sure. I understood him perfectly now. He was fearful. He was alone. He was going to miss all that he was to leave behind. He wasn't sure of what he is to find in there. I looked around. To my nostalgia tinted mind, the din and clutter looked so pretty and cute. Someone was haggling with the canteen manager. I found it funny and adorable. I got up and began to move. Maya was waiting. A friend of mine stopped me in between, grinning.

"You got into IIMA, I heard," he asked enthusiastically.

"Yeah," I nodded slowly.

"And you got the girl too," he added lecherously.

I just nodded shyly.

"*Sahi hai Bhiru! Bola ki nahin!*"

I kept nodding. This time sideways motion.

"Idiot. What are you waiting for? Oh! See, she has dropped her hanky behind. Go pick it up and tell her when giving it to her. Or may be write it on it."

I looked back. Her hanky lay there on the ground near the table I sat.

"Go, go, pick it up," he cheered. I couldn't even nod now. I trudged back, picked it and ran towards her as they clapped wildly. It was silly and embarrassing but I couldn't have asked them to stop. Till a few days back it was I who would perform such antics. I handed the hanky to Maya as we moved. Everything fell silent. I could only hear sweet tidings all around. It looked perfect. *I don't want to change a thing. Let me not do anything right now.* I decided to go back to my hometown for a couple of weeks.

To a restless heart there is no solace. While I wondered at things to come, back home reactions were a bit too strange. "Didn't you get admission in the local MBA College? Why go all the way up to Ahmedabad when you can do it here?" was my favourite. "Were you not getting promoted?" was another favourite. It didn't matter much to mom and dad. "You are okay, we are okay" was their adage. Suddenly I felt like a stranger in my own town. I came back. Narayan was getting married in Mumbai. I was to see Maya after almost a month. I was looking forward to it. She stood there in a light blue *sari*. Probably it was pink.

don't clearly remember. It doesn't matter anyway. She looked pretty. ike hell. My heart was melting. Hers had already melted. I could see t. I could see it in her eyes. She held a small fancy ladies bag in her ands, a coy, little smile inviting me. Bhairavi was also there. But she idn't matter. Actually nothing mattered. In the last one month I had oped to have erased her from my memory or at least make it fade. But uman memory is different from that of a computer. At least these days. Vith technology in fifty years, you never know. But it was now and ere. I thought of saying a few things. 'At least let her know that you nd her beautiful?' I argued with myself. But something stopped me. Vhat was it? We kept moving around the wedding ground the whole vening. Must have been a few hours. She was constantly looking at ne. Probably wanted to say something. I was waiting. For her to say it! *Vhat will I say if she says something?* I didn't want to think. It was a big rand Marwari wedding. There were a lot many items on the food menu. nd there were a lot of guests too. But we never got lost in them. We te a little and talked even less. Bhairavi was enthusiastic. She had never een a Marwari wedding. South Indian weddings are less of a wedding nd more of a ritual akin to God worship. North Indian weddings are nore than weddings. They are festivals. Maya was swooning. Where vas I? The evening went just like that. We hadn't progressed one bit. bought more time. "Let me come to the local train station with you. Vould see you people off and then go."

"Okay," Bhairavi agreed. The other person didn't say anything. She anted to hear something else.

We reached the platform. The train was about to come. I was looking l around. Anywhere but towards her. She was not ready to look away. hairavi took a break from us. She went for water or something. I had problem of where to look now?

"If you want to say something you can say it now," she said.

I had more problems now. *What do I say now?* When in doubt, dc nothing. I followed the dictum. It killed me. The train came on time It knew that the problem is not with time. I wanted someone else tc do the job for me. "Fuck you," it said.

They boarded the train and it left. I stayed back on the platform My train never took off. I bought a v*ada-pav*. It can lift you out o anything. V*ada-pav* I mean. It had the reverse effect. Made me full anc want to sit down.

Found a chair and sat down. Rubbed my thighs and yawned. I had been a hectic day and it was not over yet. I had to give many a explanations to myself. I deserved it. I needed it. It began. I had a sca A big one, near my chest, above my abdomen. She couldn't see it. N one could see it. I couldn't have shown it to anyone. It was a bit ugl actually. I placed my hand on it and it stung. I had got a call fron home. Somewhere between getting my calls from IIMs and before th interviews. It was my sister. She was laughing like mad. Something wa wrong. When you laugh unusually, something is cutting you unusuall I asked. She didn't say. I talked to my mom. She was composed. Didn ask enough about me today. Something is wrong even more. "Dad i not at home," I was told. Something was amiss. No one was telling I hung up. A little while later, in the evening I got another call fror an uncle of mine. He was dad's business partner. He wanted to kno something. "How much do you earn? And if you go for studies ho much will you be able to earn after that." Normal questions but from wrong person. I never talk about these things. Not to him. Moreove he never calls me. He broke the news. He had to. It was his money. I was gone. With the business. Dad was bankrupt. We were bankrupt. had a scar. It was ugly. I couldn't have shown it to her. Sometimes w are prisoners of our own image. Most of the time we live within th cage of our own fears. *They love this young, funny, go-getter. Who wou love you with the scar? When I don't like it to start with, what expectatio should I have from others?* I didn't trust others enough. They didn't know me enough. I stayed silent. It slithered me. Slowly, painfully, tragically. Like a carefree deer hunted and eaten by lions. I remembered chasing deer and chinkara in the zoo years before. I hadn't been able to get hold of them. I hadn't quite proven to be a lion. But the lion that fate could sometimes be, appeared to have caught on to me, in both, good and the bad way. Memories of the chase began to trickle into my mind. The numbness that I had sunk into, was slackening.

It is all because you didn't enter the lion's cage that day. He wasn't pleased with your discrimination and is taking revenge through cosmic forces.

Like hell it is. Don't be stupid. What is to happen, happens, irrespective of our efforts. It's all ordained dude.

Well, you use the word ordained and then deny cosmic forces?

It's so difficult to talk to you. I mean, well I mean, I will have to use some word, some phrase, isn't it? Else how would I communicate with you, tell me?

So, you mean, you don't believe in cosmic forces but in karma instead.

Enough buddy. Now don't give me that holy karma shit. I don't give a shit about any shit. Destiny or karma, how does it matter. What was to happen, has happened. Whatever is to happen, will happen. What can I do? I can just do, what I have to do. Right?

May be. Then why didn't you do what you could have done? I know what you would say now. You would ask me what is it that you could have done. Right?

Yeah...sort of. Tell me. You think there is something I could have done? Something that could have meant something?

Well, you could have told Maya about your feelings, to start with.

Like hell I could have. Could I have? What do you think?

Yes. I think you could have.

Hmmm...I don't know. I wish I could. But you know I am...I am...a bit scared of it not working out. I...I well don't like to own up a wish which may not get fulfilled. It leaves me heartbroken, you know.

Hmmm...yeah. I know that very well. But running away is also no a solution. You can't not develop a heart just because you are scared of i getting broken. Can you?

I know, you are right. But I don't know. I just feel her affection wil drip away if I tell her about my problems back home. I mean, I mean I get a sense that she is into me a lot more because of all this IIM an all. I mean, I must be looking like the right guy to hook up with a the moment. Right now I have pleasant memories of her. If I face th reality and it turns ugly, I don't know where that'll leave me. I migh just drop everything and go to Himalayas, for all I know.

Don't bullshit. Himalaya and all. You are too much of a sucker to eve land there. You love yourself just a teeny weeny bit too much to do that. Bu I am not sure if you are doing the right thing about Maya.

What do you suggest? You think I should go back and tell her al Bare myself out? Tell me...

Well, not quite sure of that either. If karma and destiny happen, the maybe you two will find a way to each other in some way that I can no foresee now.

Huh! Basically you are telling me to not do anything. That's th problem with you, like the rest of the world. You show me the whol circus before pushing me in with the monkeys in the end. I mean can you just come to the point directly? Holy *karma* and all! How did i all start anyway.

With the lion in the zoo.

Yeah. And what were you saying about him?

Nothing. Leave it. It's not really important.

No, no. Tell me what was it?

Nothing. I was saying that all this confusion is caused because you didn't enter the lion's cage that day. He may have got offended and...

And...?

And, connected with the cosmic consciousness to desire that just as you have left him wanting, you shall also be left wanting and waiting. You know they say, if you desire for something with all your heart then the whole universe conspires to make it come true. Maybe it does work like that. Universe shall be the same for all no, humans and animals?

O! Hello! What have you been up to? Doping? Watching Shahrukh Khan movies? You want me to believe this story???

Umm...no..just that...well may be...it's just a way to look at things.

Hmmm...Holy hell! You know how you sound right now. Don't you?

Well..like a qualified idiot.

Yes, exactly. That's what you are. A qualified idiot.

He laughed. I sniggered. Funny us. He stopped well before me. As if he could foresee something I couldn't.

11
IIMA BEGINS

The train was about to leave. Seeing any young, bright chap, I wondered if he was headed to the same place. I thought of asking a few questions but desisted lest it would appear silly. I didn't know how they will react. I hadn't known anyone from IIMA earlier. Of course other than one. Myself. But wasn't I just an aberration? I wasn't *so sure.* I was naturally optimistic but doubts lived close by. One dipped and the other took over. I was nervous about the place and the people. *God has brought me here, He must have some good plans*, I comforted myself. What could I have done about it anyway? *They selected me. It is their problem if I fit in or not.* I decided to stay myself. No one else is better qualified to be me.

I reached campus two days before the start date hoping to settle down and start studying to ready myself for the rigour to follow. Having heard a lot about it I had tried to not get affected. But it was the IIMA. The echelon of academics. Cockiness is one thing and reality another. I had to be careful.

By the first evening I had gotten my room, set it up and bought the essentials. Now I began to scourge in search of friends, the necessity to survival. I hadn't brought any. A room close to mine was open. I knocked. No response. I persisted. A lanky guy came out dressed in vest and shorts. Someone had come before me!

"Hi, I am Romal. I live in that room there."

"Hi, I am Om."

I didn't get any invitation to come inside. I hardly ever give in easily. I stood there. Conversations had dried. I saw a few books open on his table.

"What are you studying?" I enquired.

"Oh, nothing. I was just preparing for the Monday class."

"You what!!!"

This was silly. There were two days to go and someone was talking about studying! There was something so funny that it felt ridiculous. I left soon and he disappeared behind the closed doors. I heard a quick and loud bolting from inside. Was he trying to tell me something? Fuck him.

I reached the next open room. The same routine followed but this time the guy was more than welcoming. A bit too much actually. There was hardly any need to introduce myself.

"You are a *fachcha*, right?"

"What?"

"*Fachcha*. I mean first year student. You will learn soon. There is lot you need to catch up. I am Prakash. Second year."

"Okay."

"Come on in. Sit. How are you finding it? How is the whole experience?"

"It's okay." *I have hardly been here dude. It hasn't been more than a few hours.* "I just setup my room etc. Rooms are kind of small though. I expected something better from the so called best B-school in Asia Pacific, you know."

He didn't look happy with me. A wrinkle had risen up his nose.

"What did you expect? It is much better than what you have…are you from IIT?"

"Oh, no. Not at all. You?"

"I am a CA." "Chartered Accountant," he explained as I looked blank at the word. Two wrinkles. *Conversations where art thou? Humour? Intelligent remark? Exit?*

"Oh, yes. There is something very strange about that guy in the other room."

"Why, what happened?"

"I knocked on his door and he seemed more interested in studying than chatting. I mean this is stupid. Studying two days in advance. My God. I find it so funny that I can't even laugh at it."

Three wrinkles.

"I mean, in my college we studied just before exams, often just the night before. Sometimes didn't study at all. Why bother when you know studying will hardly help. Some courses used to be so tough, you know. No matter how hard you study, marks you get will be for the fact that you tried, never for solutions."

Many a wrinkles. I could hardly see his nose now.

"It is not he who is stupid, sorry to be harsh, it is you. I don't know what college you come from but this is not that college. This is IIMA and you better get cracking if you wanna just survive."

I fell silent. It didn't scare me, well a bit but I didn't want to create enemies. I was in search of friends. One down from the potential candidates. There were still a lot to go for.

As the rooms kept on filling over the next two days, I went on knocking. What did I find? Mostly men. Of different sizes and shapes with one common thing. Very focused and overawed by IIMA. Unsure of what lies ahead of them but sure of one thing. That it's gonna be tough on them and no one was sure if they would survive. I tried looking for friends in them. I found but realized friendship will take time. Everyone was so occupied with themselves that nothing else came out of them. For some it was a dream come true. For others it was a key to the money making machine. Key found, it was a matter of time, if they could just survive. But wait, there was more. It was not an end, it was a beginning. A beginning of giving wings to your ambitions. And if you didn't have any, it was time to give it a shape. Next day the class had to start. Tonight we had to prepare for the war. I was relaxed and amused at the anxiety of the people. *What can possibly be so wrong? People come every year and they do pass. We will also clear the exams. These people selected us, they must have seen something in us. No?* Well, I couldn't hear it clearly but I felt a silent sound of a doubt. All this is fine but *what if?*

That night we had a talk from the second year *tuchcha*, I had barged into the room of. He told us all that we already knew about. He just exaggerated it and dished it out with histrionics. A small blackboard was hung on the dormitory wall. He stood in front of it with a chalk. His eyes spoke of excitement as other *tuchchas* stood around, gulping water, talking to each other. Most dressed in loose tees and half pants, some in their undies. They had an exhausted look. Not from work but from sleeping. Not sleeping around, sleeping in their rooms I mean. "That's all you do in second year," they told us. And there is a reason for it.

"In first year you do not sleep," the anchor of the show roared. "It is not just another college. This is IIMA. Look at the guy next to you.

He is not just another guy. He is your competitor. Your grades depend upon how badly he does. It's relative you see."

I looked at others. *Friendship?* Whatever little was there evaporated. And there was more. There was a purpose why we were all there.

"Any guesses?" he quizzed.

"Money? Foreign jobs? I-Banks? Consulting?" I pitched in.

Cold glance.

"You want all these?"

I meekly nodded. Why not?

"Are you from IIT?"

I nodded again. In negative.

"Are you a CA?" "Oh, you are not. I remember."

"There is only one thing which can save you."

'And that is?' we all thought together.

"I-schol."

"I-schol?"

"Yes, gentlemen. I-schol. It's a rare breed. It is a word coined for rarest of rare. Coming to IIMA is just a token for the battle about to begin. I-schols are those who stand within top-20 of the batch at the end of first year." "And you...," a finger came towards me, "if you are not from IIT and you want any of those things you mentioned, you need to be an I-schol."

"And what if I don't want to be an I-schol? Just study and take what you get?" Something told me I had asked a wrong question. Some of the *tuchchas* smirked. I-schols.

Others flinched. Losers. Not I-schols I mean.

The anchor ignored my question. "You do not, want to or not want to, be an I-schol. It is not a choice. You try to be an I-schol. Whether you become or not is a separate issue. That is decided by this place which separates wheat from chaff. You don't come to IIMA. You come to a war."

Then someone asked the right question. "So what does one need to do to become an I-schol?"

"Well, there is no clear path. There are many roads to success. But there is one straight road to failure. And that is lack of ambition. Let me tell you what I did. For I am one."

Claps! Flowers! Thunderstorms! No?

I had a disturbed night. I saw myself standing on the school ground near my home. A huge army was standing in the middle of it and its commander was giving a speech. Soldiers were dressed like Romans. "Probably it is the era of Alexander where I have been transported to," I told myself in the dream. Dreams and reality are not too different for me. As the commander finished his speech, the whole army erupted in a war-cry. Their eyes were burning red. They were ready for war. The commander turned towards me. His face resembled someone I knew. "Oh, it's the same tuchcha. The anchor of the show," I howled. *So it's genetic! The warriors of that era have just become the students in this era. I was a bystander then. And what now? Hell. I need to change!* I got up. I was sweating. I got out. I found that all lights were on. I knocked on one. There was no response. I went to another. Knock. Knock. No response. Knock Knock again. Someone opened.

"Yes?" he asked. His hand still on the door. He was waiting for me to go I suppose. Quickly.

"Aa...do you have water?"

"No," he said curtly without blinking. I could see a bottle on his table.

"But I can tell you where to get it from. Go upstairs. There is a water cooler," he said easing up a little.

"Oh, ok." I turned back. He appeared better than Om. I thought asking him for something more. "Kat…kat…kattak," came the sound. Door was closed. "Kadaak. Chuiin." It was bolted. I studied all night. That wasn't enough. Everyone else also had.

Next day the classes started. It was a bit strange. This rush to be in the class on time. I had never rushed at engineering college even to be late in the class. "This is IIMA dude," said Suman running along with me. He was my dorm mate and lived next door. "I know. I know." I managed to reach in time. By one minute and twenty nine seconds exactly. No kidding. Not using this number to create humour. The door was closed and locked the next second, at one minute and thirty seconds after the scheduled time. The time was obviously as per the professor's watch. The first class went easy. Nice professor. Nice talk. But he didn't welcome us. He got straight to work. It was some random case study. He told us that everyone is supposed to speak up and there are marks for speaking. I love speaking but not in the class. I decided to stay silent and tried to give a goofy smile to the girl sitting next to me. She wasn't impressed. *Oh, so I should try and speak.* It should have been easy. I am so fucking brilliant. For the next fifteen minutes I kept trying to open my mouth but each time I had an idea, I found someone else already speaking it up. *What the hell is happening? How can they read my mind?* It began to get to me. Many people were raising hands all the time to speak up. The professor was choosing who he will let speak. When I would have an idea before others, he wouldn't look at me. By the time he did, someone else would have spoken it already. Finally he looked at me. I had raised my hand. He gestured me to speak. I froze. I had become so keen to be heard that all I focused on was to get a chance to speak. I forgot to think about what to speak. It was embarrassing. The girl next to me was laughing. I thought of kicking on her mouth. But she was pretty. I am partial to pretty girls. It is another thing that they are blind to me. The class was over but the ordeal wasn't. There was a quiz in the next class. Surprise quiz. What? Yes, that's what I said. *They can't do this to us. We have paid to study here. You can't be so hard.* I looked at others. Some had the same expression as I. Om didn't. He was beaming. He had slogged for two days for it. He already knew what's in store. Didn't he? Bastard. I got the paper. Oh my God! I knew what was in there. Last night's study had helped. Thank God for small mercies. I had a great dorm. So what if they were a little rude. In God's land everything has a purpose. Even seemingly bad things. Don't lose faith. I got busy with it. With the paper, I mean.

Next class. A different professor, same dialogues. There was no welcome-to-IIMA talk, it was all straight to work. In half an hour he completed what I had taken the whole night to break into. It was Accounts. The CAs were beaming. Engineers be hanged. It's been less than three hours and I had begun to hate the place. But I had to focus. I needed to. My hand went up to the scar on my chest. My mind immediately came to task. I asked a question. The first engineer to speak in an accounting class. All engineers gathered hope. CAs became red with shame. They passed notes. "No help to this guy," it said. It's a possessive breed, this CA. It's a competitive breed, these Engineers. IIMA has its own class culture. It was just one of them. Others we will know in time. Class was over. It was lunch time. All I wanted to do was to sleep. I began to get out but found some people were trying to get back. There was a surprise quiz again. Post class one. I died. Not nearly but completely. It was first of the thousand times that I had to die over the next few months. Okay, there was no quiz. It was a hoax. *Tuchchas* playing pranks on *fachchas*. I looked up. I had lost my sense of humour. I wanted to break someone's head. I managed with scratching my ass.

It was a hopeless place, this IIMA. It made you more competitive and took away all the fun of it. Because the fun is in winning. That's what we all were used to throughout our life. We all were either toppers or second best. Read, I said second best not second. Because there is no respect for seconds here. You study not to excel but to survive. It was a hopeless place this…

When I had entered IIMA, I had many a things on my mind. I had worries of things back home. I had thoughts about if I have left potential love in Maya because of my worries. I had memories of my over hundred friends who I needed to call or meet every now and then to feel normal. I had strange weird dreams. No, not the dreams about future. The dreams at night. My dreams used to be random. That problem was solved after I came here. There were no dreams because I hardly slept. Also I didn't miss my friends anymore. There was no time. Their memory was quickly being replaced by the hundreds of new concepts being thrown at me on a daily basis. There were eight subjects, over two hundred overly competitive students, all bright intelligent son-of-the-bitches, quizzes, surprise quizzes, assignments, results etc., etc. On top of that there were 'Oh, we are a great place to be at,' events which you must participate in. Birthdays, Friday night parties, dorm outings, unwarranted and unwanted advice of your seniors. Esoteric discussions about, 'What is the goal of life?' to 'What is your goal?' "To get married to Aishwarya Rai," I wanted to tell them. But I didn't. I stayed quiet. I wonder why! Anyway, by the time I could soak it all in, I realized half of the term was over and I was standing on the gates of the mid-term. One day sitting on the toilet seat, I happened to reflect upon my life. I had decided to bunk the class thus there was no hurry to get out. It occurred to me that being here was like being on the platform for the Mumbai local train. All you need to do is to stand there. Rest will be taken care of by the people around you. Before you realize, you will be inside the train. For mid-terms we were advised to study together, as a group. Crisis does one good thing. It can bring people together. It did that to the ten potential I-schols of my dorm. They all began to interact. Strictly professional though. We would gather in a room and discuss some particular case or a problem. Mostly two or three of us who would argue, rest would listen or try to catch the wind. I was mostly in the second lot. More class culture of the place was becoming evident to me. IIT vs. non-IIT and more importantly potential I-schols vs. nobody. Next day there was a potential macro-economics quiz. A heated discussion was on.

"No...but if the demand curve is sloping downwards and the unemployment is higher than the critical factor, in that case how can the supply increase? No way." Potential I-schol no. 1.

"It can. That is what the whole theory is about. With Government's intervention it is possible." Potential I schol no. 2.

"It is fundamentally wrong. How is it possible? I have done my B.Com with Honours in Economics. I am not boasting or anything but I know I am right."

"*Arre*, it is actually a mathematical thing. I know. Look at this equation. And I am from IIT-Mumbai, Computer Science. Believe me it is possible when the slope is towards the middle and more than 1/3. I am not boasting but well..."

Both looked at the book hard. Probably they expected the book to speak and answer. I wasn't that stupid. So thought would intervene.

"I think I know. It is actually possible," said I, slightly excited. I had a point finally.

They didn't bother to heed me. *Probably they didn't hear.*

"Hello. See, with Government expenditure the demand will go up even if locally and that would have impact on supply."

"We know that. But the problem is more fundamental." Potential I-schol no. 1 tried to wave me off.

"What is the...problem?" I asked slightly confused now. *Problem is fundamental or fundamentals are the problem?*

"*Arre*, why should the Government spend? No, no. There was a research paper published in 1987 by some professor I had read during graduation. If only I had that. I will search and then let you know," he said to the IITM Comp. science.

"*Arre*, boss. It is simple if only you would try and understand this equation. Yeah, it's a bit complicated but if you try it, you should be able to crack it with my help."

What? Me and help? Never. I am potential I-schol no. 1.

"Ummm...I guess Government will spend because there is high unemployment anyway. It may serve dual cause...," I continued.

"Anyway, leave it. We should not get stuck to something. There is a lot to cover." The topic was changed. Everything came back to normal. Some other problem, some other discussion. But the conclusion I drew was the same. To be somebody to somebody, you have to be somebody. Somebody does not like nobody. Nobody likes a nobody. I was a nobody. The I-schol was a somebody. I had to become somebody.

It had been a couple of months since I had entered the den. IIMA I mean. The pace of my life was getting decided by the rigour and requirements of the place and I had begun to feel having been left behind. I felt like a pearl necklace without the central string. Scattered. There was some momentary peace that evening. My dorm-mates had gone out for dinner. I had refused to go. Om had come to make me acquiesce. He knew me but not enough. He kept trying to reason out, I kept wiggling out.

"Why are you doing this? Why are you not coming with us?"

"Because I don't feel like. I am not feeling well also."

"Come on. You know I know you are lying."

"If you know everything then why ask. You know I don't want to go and won't go. So just go if you want to."

"This is not right *yaar*. Everyone is going. Everyone should go together. You are spoiling it for everyone by not going."

"This is too much Om. I am not asking you to not go. If you all are really so concerned then all of you shouldn't go as well. We would go when I am in the mood."

"It is not about mood *yaar*. It's about dorm culture. You are spoiling it."

"I am spoiling the culture? You create a culture for me and then ask me to do things according to it. What kind of culture is it anyway?"

"But we all do that no?"

"Because you want to. Because you like the culture. It is designed for you. In my culture no one would be forced to do anything he doesn't want to. In my culture everyone would change their plans to suit one's mood. Get me that culture and I would live according to it."

"Come on Romal. It doesn't work like that. Don't think of the dinner as just a dinner. We are creating moments here. These are snaps and talks we would remember years from now. It is all a part of the IIMA experience. Why do you not want it?"

"Because I didn't come to IIMA to get my snaps for future! I didn't come here to create moments! Moments are not created my dear Om, they are lived. We don't create moments, we get created in moments.

We do not go through our life creating moments to remember, but finding moments that make us memorable." I had become livid. I was shouting on top of my lungs. I had gotten tired of pushing him off my back. Om didn't get what I was saying but he got the message. That I would not go. Om didn't want to go like this. But he couldn't find a way up to me. Others had also gathered around my door. Jhaadu pulled Om away.

Opening the balcony door I let in the fresh air. Weariness passed through me as I sank in the chair. It had been quite some time since I had thought about the life left behind.

I stood up and looked at the bookshelf. The books looked of little use. I needed someone alive. I felt a hand on my shoulder. I shivered. I turned back, perspiring. I felt I knew the person but I had never seen him before. He looked similar to me but a lot more mature, a lot more calmer. He looked like a higher self of mine.

"Yes, I am what you think I am. You can call me Master," he said.

Three more figures emerged in the background.

"They are other sides of you Romal. A poet, a beast, and a philosopher," told the Master.

"Sides of mine? Why I never saw them earlier?"

"You did but not so distinctly. You always had multiple thoughts, didn't you?"

I remembered the conversation I had with myself when I had got the telegram from IIMI.

"Yeah, sometimes..."

"Not sometimes, many a times. You are forgetting the occasion after you let Maya go without professing your love. There have been many more occasions, you haven't noticed."

I remembered having felt something lusty and wild crawling under my skin after my selection into IIMA. *It must have been the beast. These others could be useful. This Master bloke talks sense. But he knows a bit too much. And he can read my thoughts too.* I felt threatened and encroached upon.

"*Haha.* Romal, it is no good hiding things from me. I would find it out. I am not separate from you."

"Hmmm…and why are you here today?" I made a silent promise that I would find a way out.

"Because you need us. You are close to reaching your edge. There is no one back home for you. There is no one you can go up to. And you are up against an impersonal, competitive, and tough system. You are no different from us Romal. Whatever you go through, we feel the pain too. That is why we came out today. Maybe we can help you."

"I need nobody's help. I can work on my own."

"Sure you can. But we may provide you…umm...say counsel?"

"Hmm…okay. So what do you suggest?"

"Well, I think you should focus on your studies. That is important."

"And what about…Maya."

"Not sure about that. Doesn't look like much will come out."

"Why? Why do you say so? The look in her eyes that day…"

"Ya…ya. But you didn't do anything about it then. It's a lost moment Romal. You may go chasing if you so wish. But it would take some effort. And you don't have the bandwidth. Things won't be as you left."

"Hmm…And the home front? You know…"

"Yeah, I know about it. There is not much you can do about it. Just focus on your studies. Maybe you will find another Maya. Better one maybe."

"Yeah, yeah. Maybe. Maybe you are right…"

"Not maybe…" He tried to push me.

I glared. He looked amused.

"You know, I didn't really need you to tell me all this. It all is pretty obvious."

"It always is. Obvious I mean. Most of the times. I am sure you can do it all on your own. With us on your side, it may be a little better and a little easier too. That is all we can offer. The rest is up to you."

I turned my back to them. I could sense them disappearing into nowhere. I threw a side glance. There was nothing. I turned back. I groped air where I had seen them. It felt a little warm. The air and my heart, both.

~

As the course of my desires changed, I realized a few new things. I always do. Realize new things I mean. To be somebody one has to stop being somebody to everybody. I tried. I didn't quite succeed. But I wasn't quite an I-schol yet. The smile on my face had become more occasional and frowns more likely. A good grade in quiz. I smile. A bad grade. I frown. I say something, others don't get it. I smile. Someone else said something that I didn't get. I frown. Mid-terms had been over. My grades were decent but not great.

"What did you get?" Potential I-schol to nobody.

"B-ve."

"*Arre*, very good yaar. Crack maar diya."

What good. I was expecting at least a B+ve. "What grade did you get?"

"A-ve."

I looked at him and frowned. *B-ve was good for me?*

"I know it's not good enough *yaar*. But I made some silly mistakes. Jhaadu got A+ve. He is a real stud *yaar*. I respect that guy."

OK. And what about me?

"But that's the fun of being here. Competition. Good is not good enough. Nothing is good enough. You are always on your toes. I love it. I came here for this." He quickly vanished behind other people who were matching their answers to his. You see, nobody wasn't just a lower breed. It didn't exist!

The next few weeks were exhausting. I chased the elusive elixir, that I-schol tag. There was hardly anything different I was doing now. There were only twenty-four hours in a day. I was already consuming all of it. What more I could do? Other than worrying extra. Which is what I was doing. Sometimes I felt like a stock on the Sensex. Every day was a trading day. You open up at a certain position. You close at another. You have no-idea where you are going to end up at the close of the day. When you tag your self-worth to a thing out of your control and may be outside your reach that is what you become. A commodity.

Mom had called. Things had not been looking up. What else did I expect? After the class I didn't go for lunch. Placing my hands on the desk I rested my head. Everyone was leaving. I stayed there. Everyone likes music. I like it too. But when many varieties of music are played together, it becomes noise. That is what was happening to me. I liked challenge. I liked competition. I liked adversities. But it was beginning to seem like noise now. I wanted to cry. Just a little, to ease myself. I needed silence. It was there now. I broke down. I felt a hand. It was rubbing my back.

Is it my mom? God? Dream, idiot. Oh, I didn't realize I am pushing myself so much that I have begun to hallucinate.

I started smiling. I was a little weird. I liked such weird emotions.

I got up and picked my books and began to move. She was standing just there. The pretty girl who sat next to me. I saw her just as I turned. Oh, I wasn't weird. Even though I wanted to. It's fun to be. Just a little, though. She had seen me crying. So what does she think of it? She threw a soft smile. 'It is all right,' it said. I moved towards her and kissed her on the cheek. She blushed a bit. I blushed even more. I walked away. I was smiling. She was smiling. I could see her smile without looking at her. I stopped at the door and looked back. Her face was glowing. Her black, round eyes wide in amazement. I was feeling love. It was a weird thing. I liked being weird. Just a little though. It was too much.

The days after that went even faster. There was a race. There was work to be done. I was still not an I-schol. But I was not a nobody anymore. My grades were getting better. Marginally. But potential I-schols had sensed the chemical in me. Of potential I-schol. They would ask me for tea. But my mind had now changed. I wanted to ask someone out. I had made the mistake of not seizing the moment in the past. This time I didn't want to wait for too long. But how to do that. Ask her out, I mean. I would sometimes go up to her and try to say something. Actually I didn't have to go anywhere. She sat next to me only. So all I had to do was to turn towards her.

"Varsha," I said slowly.

"Yes," she responded. Her eyes lost at me.

"Nothing."

"Okay. *Achcha*, did you get what the professor just said. You better tell me. I hardly get anything. And you have been getting such good grades."

"Oh, sure."

I could never determine her thoughts. Her face would be so blank that I would wonder if she will die of shock if I told her about my feelings. Or will she just say, "*Achcha*. That's alright. But did you just get what professor just said? You better..."

I decided to test my feelings towards her before I tested my luck. I changed my seat. It got worse. Now, I would turn back or angle to look at her. I came back. A new project had to be done for the marketing subject. I asked her if she would be my partner. For the project I mean.

"Sure," she said and vanished. She was always like that. One-second woman. Maybe she thought I was also a one-second man. Thus the blankness towards me. How can I prove her wrong? Any ideas?

We had to survey fifteen people for Dominos, our subject study for the project. It wasn't too difficult. *Ahmedabad* is a friendly place. People love to eat and talk about it as well. Especially if you are from IIMA. "Oh, you must be a genius," was the usual opening statement. But no one gave a discount to geniuses. We were hungry by the time the survey finished.

"Lunch?" she asked.

"Yeah."

"Okay. What will you have? I will have one chicken pizza and..."

"Hold on. Hold on. You want to eat here only. Let's go to some better place?"

"Sure." One-second woman.

As we ate lunch I came to know many things about her and her family. But I wasn't interested. I was interested in just one thing.

"Varsha. Tell me what do you think of me?"

Blank look for a second. "You are very intelligent. The grades you are getting...How are you managing it?"

This whole grade obsession is killing me more than ever. It is killing my love story. Hell with it. No more this hiding behind the bush business. You will have to be direct.

No, not now. Her mouth is full of food. She might throw it at me in reaction. Let me get over the summer placement. I can't afford any shocks at the moment. I will die irrespective of what she says.

12
SUMMER PLACEMENTS

Summer placements got the best out of everyone. At least everyone tried to get it ut of themselves. Our existence was measured, given shape, and then ammered to give finishing touches so that it can fit in the one page ocument called, CV, *Curriculum Vitae* for the purists. It also brings ut existential crisis and other such problems. I had mine. I always o. Don't you know better by now? I had begun to realize how lowly y existence had been before I came to IIMA. The fact that after oming here it had been completely vanquished is a different matter together. But right now I was struggling to fill in that one page with y past deeds. “I once won *Ramayana Antakshari* organized by the cal *Marwari Samaz* Association when I was nine. Will that count?” asked the I-schol *tuchcha*. He didn't consider it worthy of answering. 'lease help me. I am not able to do this myself. How did you do it in ur time? You are an I-schol. You got good summer placement too.” applied grease. He slipped. “Well. You need to find out the most gnificant achievements of your life. To start with first identify the fferent domains and then see what have you done in each.”

"Domains? Meaning?" *Drinking? Eve-teasing? Poetry? Drama?*

"Like sports, social service, performing arts, science. Anything."

"Anything?" Still nothing.

"Okay, let's take them one by one. Sports? What have you don there?"

"Well, I won a certificate of participation in *Kabaddi* when I wa in school."

"Hmm...Performing arts?"

"I did few plays in the engineering college. I got a couple of prize also." My eyes beamed.

"Hmmm...have you done anything at the professional level? Lik professional theatre or performing at some inter-college competitio at the least."

I stayed silent.

"Anything else say, presenting any research paper or working fo some social service organization?"

"Presenting a paper, ummm, no. There was no such culture at m engineering college...umm...social service...ummm...I did some a school."

"You have a certificate? Or was it some registered society? Somethin people would know? Say, Rotary Club?"

Silence prevailed. "Oh, yes. I was a member of the organizing tea during the cultural festival in our college? How about that?"

"Not worth it unless you were the head of the team."

"Head? No."

"Well, then forget it. With a CV like yours you should rather forg about getting summer placements in any I-banks or Consults."

"What if I write that I was the head? No one would know. I am the only one from my college here. Actually the first one to be here, you see." My face brightened as I filled with pride.

"The one thing you should never think of doing at IIMA is anything UNETHICAL! Get it?"

"Okay. Okay. So...what...should...I...?"

"Consider increasing font size. That is the only way you can fill the page."

Next I was visited by his successor, Om. He had a peculiar problem."Romal, tell me something, will font size 8 be readable?"

"8? That's too small. Normally everyone keeps 9. Why do you want to make it 8?" I decided to refrain from sharing my problem. I was asked to consider making font size 12.

"No, actually at 9 not everything that I have done is fitting into it."

"What?" My eyes popped out. I took his resume and began to browse through it. He had everything. Worked with an NGO, been secretary to some clubs, played as well. Not some *Kabaddi shabaddi* but something like squash, tennis type. Sports for which facilities are there in USA. He had been preparing to go to USA ever since he was born!

"Yaar, I am not sure if I can advise you on this. I mean it looks okay. Why don't you ask more people. Just take a general vote on readability?"

"No, *yaar*. I don't want others to know what I am writing. They might copy my style and use it in their CV. It's a competitive thing you know. One man's loss is other man's gain."

"Oh!" Obviously he didn't consider me worthy of his competition.

"But I can trust you. You are bright. But I doubt you have any chance at those I-Banks and consult summers. Don't get me wrong but you just don't have the credentials."

Rub it in. Rub it in. Making obvious more obvious is obscene. Didn't someone tell you that!

"*Achcha*. I will go. I think I will make it 8.5. Thanks for the advice." He left. I gave a weak smile. Another somebody to nobody talk. But I didn't care anymore about this nobody business. In my eyes I already was somebody. I had love. I thought about the moment when I would tell Varsha about my love. *How will she react? What will she say? How many seconds or minutes will the one-second lady will take to reply to it?* These were pleasant thoughts. I went to bed with them. That night I dreamt after long. Om and I stood under the dorm-stairs. He had gotten into the top I-Bank the way he wanted. I had also gotten somewhere. "I am a potential I-schol. I have I-bank summer placement. I have also become the General Secretary. I have everything. I have name, fame, and will have the money soon. *Tere pass kya hai*?" he asked.

"*Mere pass pyaar hai*. I have love," I replied.

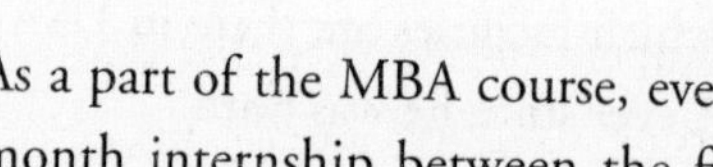

As a part of the MBA course, every student is supposed to do a two month internship between the first and the second year. Summer placement is the process to make the students do internship with various companies. Companies on their part take it as an opportunity to select students who they might want to give final job offers. Two months period will give them ample opportunity to evaluate the guy. It is also a good way to build their brand among students. The whole process is structured around 3 days, Day-0, Day-1 and Day-2. The most wanted companies, that is the I-Banks and consults come on Day-0. Indian consults and other companies like HLL, P&G etc. visit on Day-1. Day-2 sees a host of left over companies. Students are supposed to apply to companies they are interested in by submitting their resumes. Companies shortlist candidates they would like to interview. On the day of the summer placement one sees the kind of mess one may find in a stock exchange. Over two hundred and fifty commodities being traded by some fifteen to twenty traders (companies). The fate of people is decided in a matter of seconds. You get out of one interview telling them how you want to be with them without sounding desperate and even before you have relaxed you might be getting into some other interview and have to tell the same story again, with similar conviction. Why MBA? Why this career? Why this company? Would you die if you are selected? The whole juggernaut. Such a headache, I say. I didn't have to go through such trouble. Oh, no. Not because I got offer in the first interview itself. That would have been nice though, isn't it? I had no shortlists actually. Not on Day-0. Font 12, remember? These recruiters can see through such tricks. Damn smart they are I say. Om had got through it. Some I-Bank. He wasn't very happy. He was wait-listed in the other two. "Waiting list? Me? It is the companies who should be wait listed for me," he chaffed.

I could understand this competitive person very well. But I didn't understand this competitiveness. Maybe I am afraid of losing. May be that is why I don't like head to head competition. May be that is why I was losing. Oh, yes. It wasn't easy getting a summer internship. The scrutiny appeared almost as if companies have come down for the Bofors deal. I had been through several group discussions and interviews on Day-1. Over a dozen I say. I hadn't cleared any of them. I tried hard, really hard. I even tried to sell the story of me being from a small town and how I have really had to struggle hard to come here. They were not impressed. They can see through these tricks. Damn smart they are, I tell you. But that was not what was troubling me. It was but there was something else. Something was blowing me to bits. It was Varsha. My head was hanging down my neck. Hers was hanging too. But down someone else's neck. It was a guy. A guy rumoured to be her boyfriend. I don't believe in rumours. I couldn't believe the reality I saw. *So it is true. Of course. How could it be wrong?* I looked at her. I was pained. She couldn't see my love for her but could sense my pain. She walked towards me.

"You alright?"

"Oh, yeah. Just a bit..."

"Oh, it's okay. I understand. It is the summer placement. Isn't it?" She placed her arm on mine.

"Yes. It is summer placement," I managed.

She gave me a good look. *Sympathy?* "It will be alright." She ruffled my hair. They were receding. I wanted to ask her to stop. I didn't.

"I know. I was just thinking that one day, maybe a few years from now, this day won't matter. We would probably just sit somewhere around a table in a restaurant and laugh over all the chaos. I am fine. I am just thinking of that day. It better come soon." Of course I had to think of a day far away. This day looked way too far from anything I would want. Mr Philosopher at work. Take a bow, gentlemen.

She gave me that lost look again. I didn't quite like it. But I couldn't dislike anything about her. It was okay. I managed somehow.

She gave me a quick hug. "I have to go. Okay? You take care."

"Yeah."

I sank into a chair and stared at the floor. Sensing some other's gaze I lifted my head. But couldn't quite lift it. I stared at the wall ahead now. All the little and large voices that used to keep whispering to me, had gone silent. They were simmering but none was audible. As if a huge deluge of sticky glue had been thrown over them. They all had gotten lumped together and were banging on my inner walls for rescue. Bang. Bang. Bang. I could see them making impressions on the covering and taking shape against it as they tried to stand up. But they would fall soon. Collapse, bit by bit. Moment by moment. Just like me. Strength enough to barely breathe, they were dying. I couldn't witness their helplessness. Poor, weak, lonely fellows they were. Just like me. I looked up at her. Her wide smile was flashing. Her head waving. Her hairs falling on and off her face. Her hands flailing. *None of it is for me. It is for someone, not like me.* I knew all there was to know. But it didn't help. I wanted to go ahead and bare it all. Tell her what was churning inside. Spread the miserable creatures turning ugly in suffocation. But I couldn't do it. I had no strength. The sticky deluge had fallen on me too. Leaving me like the voices inside. Falling. Into an abyss like a fading star. Soon I was to be an ugly lump of burned mass, far from everyone's eyes. Alone, exhausted, and forgotten. For the first time I had found someone, just like me. But it was locked within. Just like me. There was no one to let it out. Where was that philosopher who found a meaning in every misery? Where was the poet who found a rhyme in every noise? Where was the beast who could shake himself out of every mess and tear the agony apart with its ferocity? They were all silent. I was dead meat. I wanted to cut myself and feed to dogs.

A guy approached me. *Probably he is a dog and has sensed that I am ready to offer him food.* He was assisting for the summer placement process. He was among those who had got an offer on Day-0 and was now helping their less fortunate cousins. *He must have worked with some NGO during his graduation along with so many other things. Charity begins at home, you see.* "Romal, sorry but you haven't been able to receive any offers today. You will need to be a part of Day-2. Here is a list of companies. Could you give us your preference list?" *I thought of a dog and God sent me one in no time. God always helps me. I unnecessarily crib about Him.*

"Yeah. I will."

"No need to do it right now. Give it to us tomorrow. I understand you are stressed. But hey, it's all part of the game. Cheer up buddy." He shook me by my arm.

"Yes. I know." I smiled meekly. "It's a part of the game. Yes. I understand that you understand."

He hurriedly left. I couldn't get myself up. I wanted to be transported somewhere. Somewhere unknown, where I would be a stranger. Where there would be some peace. Some solace. I wanted a little solace. But all I had was chaos of people jostling with each other to check their results, and those who already knew their results were discussing it with others. Winners were telling their tales, sometimes with pride, sometimes with humility. Losers were licking their wounds, sometimes with grudges, sometimes with brevity. Part of the game, I say. I trudged outside. It was hot and burning. Reaching my room I sat in front of the computer and logged into a chat room. Nothing interesting. I sent 'Hi' messages to a few. No one replied. I told them to fuck-off. They still ignored me. Sometimes none of my tricks work. It was one of those moments. I was in an unknown zone. I took off my clothes and lay on the floor naked. Sun rays entered from my balcony and warmed my body. I let them caress me. The rays were getting filtered by the tree leaves in front of my room. They were playing hide and seek with me. I joined in. I twirled and twisted my body to let the rays touch. I changed postures. So did they. It began to tickle me. I giggled. Soon I was laughing. For what reason, I didn't understand. Sun had begun to set. I was again with myself. I went back to my computer. Waited for someone to say 'Hi'. None did. It doesn't matter whether I go to them or not. They never accept me. No one ever misses me. I felt a little quake. The poet had got its breath back. Like in a trance, I began to type,

across the sea…

in the blue end be

a little solace ...
in a lonely place
with trees so dark
with glowing bark ..
leaves which glisten
as I listen
sounds of heart
pounding so fast
as I cross
roads so crass
leading to an end
then having a bend
as I walk
the lonely path
I shun the world
purge the mind
drew the blind
as I kneel
over the pond
and plucked some water
between my palms
and in it were you
looking at me .

I turned behind

only to find
a distant hill
beyond the chill …
and I rushed
with all my might
having the distant
knoll in sight
trees cried
so did the sea
don't go, don't go
O' wanderer knight
but possessed I was
with your only sight
I jumped the tree
and crossed the sea
only to find
everything but thee
and I sat
gasping for breath
as I longed
a little solace
in a lonely place

After purging itself out, the poet felt calm. It went back to sleep. The philosopher had vanished in some cave that I didn't know about.

I didn't miss him much too. If I could, I would purge him altogether. But I couldn't. I went to purge what I could. To piss. I splashed water on my face. My eyes were red and moist with the water splashed. *A few heartbreaks can't break me down.* The beast had begun to vibrate now. Slowly I felt it shrugging the debris off its body. It was yet to regain ferocity. It was still seething with the hurt. It needed a kick. There was a party that night. I took it there. Loud music was on. People were huddled in groups. They said 'Hi' to me. *Finally someone said that.* I waved back and kept walking. Head down, mapping the floor, I entered a room. They offered me a drink. I let it pass. I was looking for something else. I heard laughter from the next room. I headed for that. She was sitting there. Varsha. Dressed in a black *salwar* with a reddish brown *kameez*. Her *dupatta* was missing. I looked where it was. I soon found it. He was wearing it. The guy not like me. She was sitting in his arms. For a moment I felt she was flustered. I gave a meek smile. Just when I was to go, he called me. You know who. He took me for a drink. I couldn't say no. We were practically related. By the bond of love. Not for each other though. After a couple of bottoms-up, I came back. She was still there. Now with a book. In the middle of all the chaos, she could concentrate on a book. I wanted to ask her which book it was. I couldn't. I sat on a chair instead. After a while she asked me.

"What are you doing? You look quite sad. Still not over the summer placement fiasco?"

How well she knew me! I moved up to her and sat close by. "No, not quite. Well kind off." My eyes were still lowered. *If I look up will she be able to see my vulnerability? Will that reignite the chaos I have managed to rein in somehow?* I looked up at her and quickly looked away. Her eyes were shining with a thousand stars. Each lit with a moment of future she could foresee. And none of it had me. The beast sank again. "Yeah, may be. Or maybe I am just tired." I collapsed on the bed. My head close to her feet. Even in such a state I hadn't forgotten creating scenes from Bollywood movies. Bollywood goes deeper in me than the beast, the poet, and the philosopher. She ruffled my hairs. The beast jumped and gave a violent cry, before it came back, wanting to be tamed, licking her feet.

"I love you." I said holding her hands. She laughed. He came back. You know who. "What happened?" he asked. I was still holding her hands. I hesitantly eased it.

"Nothing," she said, still giggling.

"Tell me what happened?" he asked curiously, sitting close, patting my back.

"Romal is telling me that he loves me."

"HaHa. I told that to Shyamini too. After two drinks I guess guys can love all the girls. Isn't it my *dost*?"

A warm smile came to my face despite of myself. I couldn't help giving in.

"Yes. And I guess after two more pegs we would start raping them. You better watch out baby."

"Haha. That is how I like you Romal. Lively," she said and gave me a hug. Bollywood had completely taken me over. I and 'you know who' went for more drinks. I wanted to lose myself completely. I drank like a fish. I know that's an old saying. But I am too drunk to try new lines. None of them work anyway. After drinking, I was dancing. I don't know what I was doing. Not that anyone was watching. Everyone was like that. Oblivious of themselves. I wanted to be just like them. I kept dancing till I fell on the floor. I woke up to find that the night was about to end. A new dawn was about to come. Gathering myself I walked out. Stumbling into those who were still asleep. On the floor. Over the stairs. Under the fast fading dark sky lit with stars, under the influence of last night's nectar, still recovering from the fiasco that was yesterday, I kept walking. With the new dawn a new set of questions were born. Answers were still far.

Do I really love her? Or I just need her? Didn't I see in her the rope to bind the various me? The passionate and ambitious man. The desirous and wild beast. The sensitive and gentle poet. The detached philosopher. She could play a lover to the man. Master for the beast. Inspiration for the poet. The philosopher could live by himself. He doesn't seem to want anyone anyway. And I don't like that guy anyway. Philosopher I mean. Didn't I need her to be the anchor to my constantly rocking self? To be the assurance to my doubtful self? The centre of my existence which I sorely missed? Or all this is bullshit and she is just my ticket to a better life? A small town boy trying to get a foothold in a glossy world. An on campus girl-friend can enhance your reputation and visibility, you know. And can add some juice to your days at IIMA. Which otherwise take the juice out of you. Till I get the Aishwarya and Sushmita of the world, I need to carry along with something no. They are also having affairs anyway. Do I not feel cheated when I read about them in the newspaper? But I keep quiet. I keep my peace. I wait for my time. I have a philosopher on my side you see. He helps me at such times. When I have to wait I mean. Till then she could fill in their shoes. Varsha I mean.

Such a lame trick I say. But I am kinda cheap, didn't I tell you. I asked the various me. My counsel. Their advice hardly ever worked but I had to ask them nonetheless. It's a strange relationship I had with them. It is a struggle to live with so many contradictory selves who do not even like each other. That is why sometimes I think I should not do any work. It is so much work just being me. I just want to laze on a nice beach with maybe a martini in my hand. And it would be good if I could get a few bikini clad models to ease the headache these others within me cause. I particularly like the Kingfisher calendar ones. But I shall do with some lesser known ones too, if Kingfishers ones are out of stock. But just make sure their waist is not more than 22". Okay, 24" will also work. But not more than that. Nothing doing. I have certain standards *yaar*. But people do not get it. They do not understand my needs. They do not understand why I am often exhausted and haggard even though I have been sleeping for many hours. What would they know what is it to be me! More on that later. It was time for others to speak. I shall be on a silent mode for a while. Click. Tape on the mouth. The beast spoke first.

"All I know is that you want her dude. Everything else is irrelevant." He quickly ran off. He didn't like to be ignored. He knew I would ask others' for advice. He didn't like others. He was a man of action. Sorry, animal of action. Whatever.

I looked at the poet. He stayed silent but his head gave a gentle nod. A soft smile lit on his face. His eyes had a radiance. She had given him inspiration for quite a few poems. He was happy with her. Even if it meant my happiness was getting fucked. My world was constantly under quakes. It didn't matter to him. *Such stubborn people are poets. Self-centered and selfish. And sometimes selfless too.* I didn't understand them. These poets, I mean. The philosopher sat silent. I didn't want to look at him.

He would tell me something I do not want to hear. "Your time will come, life is long. How does it matter whether you love her or need her, when she is not into you. Love is not one sided after all. Such is life. It happens to everyone. Take it as an experience life has to offer, it shall help you grow and become a better man." Or some such shit. Of no use they are, these philosophers I tell you. They know everything but understand nothing. They have answers for everything but cure for nothing. Useless, useless, useless, I say. Now see what he is suggesting.

'It is useful to have a few useless things around. It makes you value the useful even more. And what you value, you nurture.'

Huh. I can't deal with him. Just take him away. Takhliya.

Dismissing the counsel I sat in the middle of the field. My head bent low, sunk in my chest. Slowly my mind began to go blank. And he surfaced. The Master. I didn't look up but could feel his heat. I could feel his warm, considerate smile. He was unlike the others. He was considerate without being condescending. He knew I was too proud to take condescence. He was warm without being patronizing. He knew I was too independent to like that. He would give what I needed without my asking for it. He understood me. He gently touched my hair. I sank my head further. He held me by my cheek. I began to sob. I grabbed his hand. It was soft with freckles on it. He had experienced the tumult of life but had not lost his warmth. He still had faith. He still had the strength of reason, of conscience. War torn but not weary. I wet it with tears. His hands, I mean. I became hysterical. He offered me his hanky. I stuffed it in my mouth. He waited patiently. I sobered down.

"You need to move on. Your family needs you, remember. Focus on your studies," he advised.

"I will try."

"Not try. I want you to do it. You have to do it. You will have to do it. Don't you want to be a big, bad boy, haan? Don't you want to rule the world, haan?"

I stayed silent.

"And don't forget the girls you can get. The American, Nigerian, Hungarian, all kind. And even the Ugandan. Like your engineering friends said you should," he cajoled me.

I quick smile came to me before it sank in the quicksand of moroseness. I understood him. He was too pushy. He would never back down from what he has suggested until you prove him wrong. And I would not have won him in this argument.

He understood my silence. I was angry at fate. Master hasn't been able to get me anything by now. All my hard work had gone in vain. I was nowhere in studies. Summer placement had gone awry. My love life was nipped in the bud. Lost before it could take shape. I already had troubles at home. I didn't want to heed his advice anymore. He understood his limitations too. There was nothing he could offer me as of now, other than advice which was of no worth. He knew it very well. He did what he could in the situation. He vanished. Damn smart, I say.

I looked up at the sky in anger. "Do I deserve nothing? Am I a dog? You fucking son of a…" I howled and spat. At whosoever sat up there. I had begun to lose my faith in Him. It was just a bit too unfair, I say. It came back and fell on my face. The spit, I mean.

13. SET ME FREE

Angels and Demons: Joint meeting

Mentor angel and demon sat in the board room. News clippings of the recently launched channel, *Direct Earth Se*, were being shown on the projector screen. "A young boy had spat skywards somewhere in *Ahmedabad*, in angst against the rottenness of the system and fast deteriorating management", the channel decried. "The world was better managed under the socialist regime till a few decades back. A bit slow but more humane. The advent of new corporate project based management system hasn't done any good. It is more efficient but rotten. No denying the truth. It highlighted the fact that the trend has become more apparent ever since some of the officials of earth tainted *Enron* and its auditors have joined post the spate of suicides by its employees a few years back. Is it time to ask for a change in the system? Finding scapegoats and sacking a few may diffuse the issue for now. But what about the larger question of..."

Mentor angel switched off the television. "Such a fine mess we have gotten ourselves into, I say. Why the hell did you people had to select the same guy for your tricks? Couldn't you go somewhere else? It's violations of rules," he shouted.

"Cool down. Cool down. Violations of rules, you say? Who was trying to have our pleasure by your own tricks? Did I ask you to do that? Did I? Did you file for permission with my department for that? Did you?" mentor demon roared.

"All right. All right. We did not follow the process to the hilt. But come on, let us admit. No one ever does. I mean, it was just supposed to be a trainee project. This guy here was new, he was excited and I just didn't want to break his heart. That's it."

"Whatever. It's a mess all right. And we got to do something about it. No use throwing filth at each other."

"Actually it would all have been okay if this love angle would not have crept in. How did that happen? At least I didn't plan that thing," trainee demon finally spoke.

"Neither did I," trainee angel quickly clarified. Both looked at each other suspiciously before looking at their mentors for answers.

"Ah, no. You don't plan these things. This is one of those things which we don't decide. This fucking, sorry for the cuss word, may Lord forgive me. This thing love is actually upon humans. They decide it. And often even they don't. Actually we are still looking into this subject. Many studies and research have been conducted but no conclusion has been reached yet."

"Hmmm...," all of them chorused. A grave silence filled the room.

"We need to give him something. We need to do something about it. Question is what?" Mentor Angel spoke.

The two mentors locked their eyes as an idea hit them simultaneously. An agreement was reached.

The summer placements day had gotten over. It took just as much time as it takes for a day to go by though quite often it crawled. I had got somewhere. It didn't really matter where. Okay, it was a marketing company. "I always wanted to check marketing as an option. It's something I would like to evaluate and see for myself if I can like it," I tried to convince myself as I told about it to one of my dorm *tuchcha*. Not the I-schol one. He had no time for me anymore. It was my potential future. An almost nobody. He listened to my passionate speech about how I never really wanted to be in any of the I-banks and consults and in a strange way God has chosen what was in my best interests and my real desire. And how...how... He gulped more water from his bottle as I got lost in the dorm television as Sachin had just hit a four. It wasn't really Sachin and I guess there was not a four or something but there was something on television which caught my attention. Just that Sachin hitting four is the most commonly used line for cricket in India. I am an Indian. A proud one. I had reasons to be. No one abroad wanted me anyway.

"It happens...it happens...," the nobody tuchcha said.

"What happens...?"

"When God gives you lemon you suddenly find love for it. Also discover it has so many health benefits." He threw a sly smile. I gave one back and broke into a wide smile. A new wave rose in my head. It always does. Like a halo effect, it did something. One note rose within me and it brought many others. I wrote one poem around it. It didn't make me feel better but a little lighter. *Someday am going to trash all those poems. I really will. All I do when I get trashed is write poems.* The thought made me break into a loud laughter. I broke into an impromptu song and dance number. I got up and did a little funny jig. Funny, just to me. I felt as if a hole has been created into my dark head and someone is screaming from that hole. I could hear him distinctly. *Fuck it man. Let's do it man. Come on man. Will you just let a bad day at summer placement kill your spirit man? Will you let one girl make you lose your heart man? You are much better than that man. God has thought of bigger, grander things for you man. We have been created for God's pleasure man. He is to fuck us and we need to keep smiling. Forgot about that man? Now my man, gimme a smile here man. Lookie here friend, up in the mirror. Take off that dull look off your eyes man. No good they are to you man. Forget about those fellows man. The futile poet, philosopher, and the lame beast they are I say. You are beyond them man. You have a spirit too man. Use that man. Show me those lovely rose petals. Show me some of that mischief man. You haven't had a bad dream in a long time man. May be it's time to have one. Let's go to sleep man. To hell with the world man. It goes on man. Let's go and continue sleeping man. No one achieved anything great remaining awake man. At least you didn't man. Sorry for that man. Fuck everyone man. Time to bed man. Sweet dreams man. Fuck yourself in there man. You haven't got anyone else man. Have nightmares man. Good luck man. I love you man.*

All was forgotten once I got up from a deep sleep. I might have been visited by some nightmares but I didn't remember any. I did have faint memories of having been visited by the Master. I remembered having farted at him. That is what he always did, farted. I gave him back this time. I had decided to unshackle myself from the expectations, from the desires, from my many wandering thoughts about future. From the poetic impulses, philosophical musings and futuristic ambitions. I decided to live for the moment. To let go of what was not to be and move on to what could be. Life began to move fast. There was nothing to reflect upon and even less to ponder. Life was to bear fruit out of seeds I had sown and I had no control over it. Sometimes not having any control is such a boon. I began to form many friends now, mostly nobodies. Somebodies didn't even have time for themselves leave alone nobodies. Life was a staircase to them and on a staircase there are no breaks, only beginning and ends. In between there are counts about number of steps one has climbed. All steps look the same, just the count differs. What a silly, stupid life. Sad, it was not mine. Hey, just a passing thought. But I was having fun. You don't need to fill pages telling that. Just a simple, short statement is enough man. Go have a ride man.

After autumn comes the spring. And spring is the season of nightingales. A set of nightingales had descended upon the campus. French girls. IIMA has an exchange system with foreign colleges. Foreign students come to our campus to add some colour to its brick and mortar existence. The ones we are most interested in are girls from France. Being a girl is enough but being from France brings an element of fantasy to it. Suman and I had joined the exchange club. In the interview for the club membership I claimed to have a lot of computer programming experience and how I intend to use it to build a website for the exchange club. Suman also faffed something to the same effect. Of course everyone knew the real motives. For the next couple of weeks we selected the birds we had to net sorry help form nest and told them details about how to live in India and whom to meet and all. When enquired about the weather we told them that it is always very pleasant here especially with the right company but they sent us online weather reports proving to be otherwise. Such arguments always lead to better things is what Suman and I convinced each other. Such innocuous topics of discussions soon fizzled out and we waited for their arrival so that our relationship could be rekindled. The fateful night happened to be the one preceding our end term examinations and keeping the IIMA tradition, Suman and I were burning the morning oil that is at 3 am we were rubbing the question book against our head hoping for something to filter through. Mr. Secretary was roaming in the corridor wearing nothing but shorts and rubbing his chest to eradicate any possible growth of flora and fauna there. We slowly pushed the door closed lest the pest (read Secretary) sneaks in and freaks us out. A few hours before the examination there is hardly anything one can do to improve your situation but there sure are antibodies to kill whatever little enzymes are remaining in your body. Exposure to high powered radiations from Secretary was one such thing. They could annihilate whatever self-confidence you might have created by solving the preliminary questions. Just like I had a switch (once upon a time, was under repair post-arrival in that red brick institution) which got activated on telling me what I cannot do, Secretary had many switches which kept getting activated at any activity random or sane. We heard loud knocks on our door and panicking got under the blanket. The door was pushed open and we were exposed to an over-heated Secretary with sweat irrigating the potential flora and fauna space and trickling down to well hopefully actual flora and fauna.

"Yaar, close that alarm of yours. Why have you put that on when you are already awake?"

"Oh, yes. Oh, yes. Sorry forgot," Suman mumbled.

"It unnecessarily disturbed me and others."

"Oh, actually I had put it on to know when to sleep. You know it's important to sleep well before exam," I smarted.

A quick glare and marching boot is all I got. I could sense that my SCM (self confidence meter) had dropped marginally but the quick response had saved it from potential savagery.

Suman and I quickly got ready, for the alarm meant the landing time of the migratory birds was an hour away. We had to be there with a watery smile, day old garland, and heart full of desires. The flight was on time. My mind was thinking in rhyme.

One two three

One with two free

One is like Madhubala

Other looks like Sri

They came soon. There were four of them. We rejected two. They looked small. *Can take care of themselves.* We focused on large ones. I chose the thinner among the two. Suman was muscular and thick set. *Heavier one for him.* We put them in the auto and squeezed ourselves in. Suman and I gave knowing smiles to each other. We had to wait for our time. They didn't smell too good. Due to the long flight, we reasoned. Soon we were below the dormitory. We helped them alight. Stairs were long and circuitous. We took it upon ourselves to take them onto their room on second floor.

"Sorry, there are no elevators here," we told lifting them.

"No…no…no…it's okay. Please put it down. We will carry them ourselves." Bags, they meant. That's what we were carrying all along. We didn't know the French as well as they knew Indians. We insisted and dropped the bags upstairs. We shared a few smiles and left.

Next day the exam got fucked. We always wanted a fuck and got it. Huh. Heading into the mess, they spotted us.

"Listen, we were hoping to go out for lunch today. Would it be possible for you two?"

Possible, they said? My head swung like a puppet but they were looking at Suman. Damn it. I craned my neck. Suman seemed as if a bomb has been placed in his hand.

'What's the problem?' my eyes asked him.

Oh! I understood. *Tomorrow is the exam and he wants to study for. As if that would matter.* Often we work just to absolve ourselves of the impending results. He left us with his tail between his legs. He knew he was being an idiot. But sometimes being an idiot is not a choice, it's your nature. Haven't I known one for so long? I had a delicious lunch. The girls paid for it. God was really great at times. He just doesn't tell us when he is going to be. My fetish for *Judaism* had been my best investment so far. It had paid at the IIMA interview. It was paying now. One of them was a Jew. *Hallelujah! L'Chaim!*

God is what connects all of us, goes the saying. I believed in it now. Religion was the bridge between us.

Many more lunches and dinners ensued. My knowledge of *Judaism* was increasing with every night. Oh, no! Not through direct lessons. I studied on net at night to discuss the same in the day. IIMA had never looked better. Days and weeks just flowed by like lotus in water. What does that mean? I don't know *yaar*. Just figure something by yourselves, will you? I am going into private space of sort and I am losing interest in making it enjoyable and comprehensible for you, you see. Anyway here it goes. Secretary still roamed thumping his measly chest. I wondered if it will vanish all together. *Tuchchas* still wandered up to my room to warn and scare me of the impending mountains to be climbed. Placements next year they meant. "I have long since lost interest in geography," I told them. They foretold my fate from the symptoms. I shut the door at them. I had God on my side now.

She was inside my room. I shut the door. "Insects."

She sat on the bed, holding a book and drew the quilt. I had one good look at her. She was petite, fair and with a touch of ammonia colour could become blonde. Specs made her a little coy. She didn't have that cold and objective look some of the foreign girls could have. Or the too erudite ones have. Those who know too much. She still looked like the girl. The kind I liked. Her finger slid on the book. My hands slid on her waist. Hmmm…so I wish. I find girls anyway inscrutable.

And foreigners! *Best way to know the results is to try it.* Thoughts of Varsha visited me. I felt being disloyal to her. Amused, I smiled at my stupidity.

"What happened?" she asked. Her voice laced with concern.

"Nothing." I brushed aside Varsha and the quilt to sit next to her.

My feet touched hers. She didn't move. I did. Taking the book from her hands and specs from her eyes I kissed her. She remained still. Then she responded. Quilt fell on the floor. I on top of her. She banged her head on my table. We broke into laughter. I pushed my hand inside her tee. She giggled. I put a hand under her head. She giggled a bit more. She began to kiss me on the throat. I closed my eyes. Varsha's face flashed. I opened my eyes, touched her back and felt her thigh. She turned around. The moment fell still. I got up.

"What happened?"

"Let me put off the light."

I lingered near the switch board, put them off and turned around. My heart was pounding. It had begun to talk in French. I didn't know what it was saying. It wanted me to ask her to leave. The gnawing reality which I had long been sensing but was hoping to be untrue had become clear. That somehow or the other, intentionally or unintentionally, without my knowing, Varsha had moved to the centre. She had gotten closer than anyone else. Like a piece of hot, molten lava passing through a pool of water, she had slipped through my emotional core. Me, the emotional me! Singeing it, simmering it, hitting the nerve centre and sticking up to it. I had never witnessed such a feeling before. Maybe it was because of the love-hate game angels and demons were playing. Maybe it was because I had been left emotionally vulnerable. Maybe it was because of the competitive stress this place brings. I don't know. Her presence, and awareness of it was not letting me sleep. Neither with myself nor with anyone else. Indian or foreigner. And she wouldn't allow me to sleep with her anyway. Such a selfish bitch she was I say. But it was not just her. I remembered my hesitation with Garima earlier. The lock I had felt that night. It was the shy poet who was holding me back. He didn't want to make an effort, looking for that poetic, dreamy, soft love, this self-conscious self of mine. He wanted the moment to unfold on its own, consuming the two of us, inflamed by our innate desire and bound by a seamless yarn. Such a damn loser I say.

There was another sound. Someone was banging my door. Then there were many.

"What happened? What is it?" I shouted.

"*Abbe*, open the door." It was Suman.

"Suman, not the best of times. Let me sleep. Later."

"*Arre*, open the door. Now that you have become big-shot, you won't even talk to us?" came another voice.

Secretary? A somebody acknowledging nobody? World can't be the same. Hailey's comet may have crossed it after 76 years.

"You okay with opening the door?"

"Yeah," She said dressing up.

Opening the door I got out. Rattled, I showed mock anger. Their faces were beaming. They threw me on the bed and leapt over, banged me with their fists and shouted, "*Abbe*, you have become an I –schol! You have broken into top-20!"

"What?" I said.

"Yes. Bastard," they said.

"Please get off me. I can't breathe," she said.

14
MAN AND THE MONKEY: HARDLY ANY EVOLUTION

Poets have a peculiar problem. They want what they want, nothing else. Once a poet wanted a piece of paper for writing his verse. Near some poetic place he began to cry. A thief with a noble heart saw poet cry and his heart melted. He had a bag full of currency. Keeping it near the poet's feet he left. Such a nice person he was. He didn't even want to be acknowledged for it. You may say it's a story. It doesn't happen in real life. Robin Hood doesn't exist. You will be surprised by what all can happen in real life. Once I met a bank robber in a train. He was so afraid of his mother that he wouldn't smoke in front of her. He put the cigarette in my pocket and asked to meet him at the compartment gate after some time. I thought he is fooling around. But the moment he got up his mother checked his pockets. She knew he is going to smoke. She was pleased with her child's cleverness and disappointed in his habits.

Let's come back to the poet. The poor guy is already so sad. He opened the bag, looked towards the sky and howled, "You never send me what I need at that moment. When I was dying of hunger you gave me poetry. Now when I want to write, you give me currency? I just want plain sheets of paper. What will I do with these? Take them away." He threw the bag away. He threw them into the sea or down the hill depending upon whatever you feel is the right kind of poetic place. Use your imagination there. Similar was my condition. When I was trying to be an I-schol, I couldn't make it. Now that I was one, I didn't know what to do with it. I didn't want it. I had already made plans for life without its burden. It looked like a noose. I tried to live with this new found status symbol like a monkey who given a dagger hurts himself. Some things were welcome, like admiration from friends and strangers. Others were not. Like newfound expectations from myself. I wondered if it can bring me love. But it failed the acid test. Varsha did say once that she didn't know I was I-schol material. Hell with this material business. She just didn't know way too many things about me. I began to study harder to justify the rank. It sank. One night I again had a dream after long. I was hanging from a rod. The rod was hanging from the clouds. I was high in the sky but was slipping my way towards mother Earth. But that was not enough. I looked down only to find that a pointed steel rod is awaiting me. I got up before I really fell though. I always do. There were more such dreams that began to visit me frequently. I will tell you about them later. Actually I will never tell you. Forget about them. I too have.

I began to run. Literally and figuratively. I stopped studying hoping that I would drop out of this I-schol business. And I took up my old love, running. Do what you love and you will get more love. Varsha also used to run. We began to meet often. I wasn't too happy about these encounters. It would always leave me rudderless. I would form new strategies to deal with meeting-her-after-effects. Nothing worked. But conversation with her showed me something. We were different. Like our running pattern. She ran on a road, which went somewhere. I ran in a ground, in a circle. Crossing over the same point again and again, tirelessly, hopelessly.

The first year got over. Summer internships began. I had mine in Mumbai. Varsha was there. So was Suman. He lived in a fancy company guest house. We would gather there to beat the heat. One Sunday afternoon Suman and I met Teen Deviyaan of our batch. The wannabe who could hide it, the wannabe, and the wannabe who couldn't hide it. We were to watch a movie. The room had two beds with a mattress thrown in between. The wannabe who could hide it lay on one bed with one of our batch mates. Wannabe who couldn't hide it immediately slipped in with Suman on the other bed. He looked at me and winked. I lay on the mattress in between. The middle category, wannabe, happened to be Varsha. She was changing her dress in the bathroom. She was actually just taking her clothes off. She came out wearing a shorts and a thin t-shirt. Suman looked at me, his expression saying, lucky bastard. I was hoping she would slip in with the other two wannabies. But her sole purpose in life looked designed to make me uncomfortable. She asked me to give her some space and spread herself. I could feel her thighs. It was bliss. I forgot all my worries. Such is effect of love, you see. Sorry! Closing my eyes I secretly prayed that the effect on the inside should not get reflected on the outside. It didn't. But I lost my faith soon and walked out. There was a sea nearby. How far can you go from the sea in Mumbai? How much can you run from yourself? Forever. I sat on the sand. It was wet. Stuck on my clothes. Like this I-schol thing had stuck, suffocating me. All the big companies were now within my reach. But I didn't know if I wanted to be there. I had consulted a Tuchcha once. He drew a risk-reward graph. Showed where various options stood on it and proved that I-banking was the most optimal solution. It looked something like below.

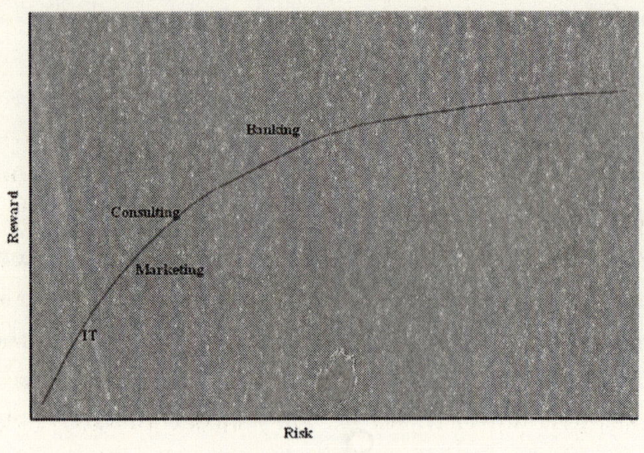

I was amazed. He should be authoring a book title, 'Human problems made easy'. Human problems have only one source of solution. Human. You are the cause, you are the effect. I probed within. May be I can be there for two years, earn some money. Would help family too. I tried to justify. I wasn't fully convinced but it looked an okay deal. I didn't know what I wanted to do if not this. Or was too scared to see it and admit. "You are just running away from responsibility which talent brings," said the Tuchcha. Running came easy to me. But what would he know. I looked up. There were dark clouds in the sky. Nothing could be seen beyond them. Beyond them were the stars for me to gather. I wanted to embrace them in my arms. But I would have to wait. I decided to wait for the sky to clear up. Literally and figuratively. I decided to let the fate decide. I would just trudge along. Life has brought me this far. It will take me a little bit further too.

Beginning of a new season. It was time for the farmers to sow seeds, for grass to turn green, for birds to chirp, for a cuckoo to lay eggs in its own nest. For India to become friends with Pakistan? Well no, that's a bit too much in any season. I was far away from all this. It was time for me to sleep. It was the beginning of second year of MBA. Harvest was far. Sowing had been done. I was an I-schol. Jobs were my bapauti. Recruiters were my concubines. I had taken a course with classes in the evening. It interfered with my sleep time. I dropped the course. I never let anything interfere with my goals. My goal was to compensate for the lack of sleep in the first year and build up inventory for future years of sleeplessness that admission to IIMA and I-schol status had bestowed upon me. I am tempted to say that it was like a cross and I was close to Jesus Christ. Actually I want to say I was Jesus Christ. But first version is too much and second one is far too much. May Lord forgive me for the sin I couldn't commit. Though not as bad as the first year, second year was not without its evils. The fear of courses and flunking had been curbed but a new demon had raised its ugly head by now. Placements! Pre-placement talks! Meetings, discussions, case-contests, CV points, business fests, marketing fests, operations fests, fests, discussions, fests! There were a few categories which were not affected by these. Those who had made the choice and those who had no choice. Some had got job offers based on summer internships performance. They formed the first breed. Life was sex, booze, and party for them. Of course arranging that was left to them. In life we all have to take responsibility for ourselves. Huh! Second was formed by people who didn't have much hope and didn't care much either. Life was sex, booze, and party for them as well. With the same disclaimer. Haha! Then there were the leftovers. Like me. It was akin to being in the middle of the sea with a wooden plank. The sea is too large to swim across. The plank is too small to make a boat. I was in a huge tank of H2 and O2. Hydrogen didn't let me live and oxygen wouldn't let me die. The plank would keep me afloat. The sea would suck me out. I was an I-schol. It kept me in the fray. I had nothing else. I wasn't assured of my chances. Life could be sex, booze, and party for me too. But I would have to slog to become eligible for it. Of course once I become eligible then I would be told of the next punch line, 'It is yours if you can arrange for it.' Fuck offfff. I had decided to choose sleep over pre-placement talks and such antics.

My glorious sleep was interrupted by a sudden knock on the door. As a rule no one in my dorm would normally do that. They knew their and mine culture code varied and the only thing common was that they were always different. I got up, armoured myself with a white vest and ventured out to check who had breached the moral code of conduct and found two people in black suit, combed hairs and rimless specs. I looked at them as if they are from Mars and they stared as if I am from a black hole. The scene was similar to a meeting between a well fed, roped, domesticated dog meeting its street version. They both wanted to say a lot many things but did not know where to start.

"Umm…we are looking for Romal's room. Someone told me this is the one." They started.

"Yes. It is."

Silence.

"Give me a sec." I got in, got dressed and reached for the door again. Opening it I invited them in.

"Hi. I am Romal."

Handshake. "Hi. We are from Mckinsey." They had bought a t-shirt from the institute store. "It's lonely at the top," it said. I looked at them blankly. We were still two different breeds.

"Actually we were holding a discussion today and wanted to meet all the guys who are in top-30 of the batch. But you were not there…"

"Oh, yes. Actually, I wasn't feeling, well, very well…" Lame excuse.

"Yeah, we figured that. So we thought we would come and meet you. Didn't want to miss the chance of meeting a superstar." My eyes widened. Smile broke on my face. Their eyes twinkled. They knew how to break the shell of egg.

"Well, you are. You are an I-schol. Not everyone can claim to be that. It's a difficult thing to achieve. I couldn't in my year. But here, this fellow, he did." He sat on the chair while the other fellow, the old I-schol stood and smiled. Egg and shell. Nothing had changed.

The duo from McKinsey were there to "pick my brain". That's what they had said. Instinctively, I clasped my head lest they pick it out.

"Headache," I sheepishly said realizing what they meant.

The room got filled with grave intentions and serious mood. The fan moved awkwardly, I rested against the wall and looked around restlessly before halting on their faces time and again. They surveyed my bare room. It wasn't organized but with the limited items I kept, there was not much scope to be messy.

"You remind me of my days," said the I-schol of the two.

"You were even more nerdier," replied the other one.

Nerdier? What the hell does he mean.

They gave me a small talk on how they are filled with distant familiarity, nostalgia, and all such nice, noble, and tender emotions. Basically they tried their level best to appear human, simple, and the guy-next-door. I played my part and feigned interest. Nod. Smile. Nod. Awkward shuffle. Nod.

"So Romal, what's the plan?"

"Plan?"

"I mean what do you intend to do with life?"

Blank. Blank. Blank. Live it?

"Hmmm…I see."

I could see where it was heading. Bastards had come to brain-wash me. They didn't know there wasn't much to wash. I had sent it out for dry-cleaning. I could see their game. They were about to begin a Good Cop/Bad Cop routine. I wasn't up for it. It was just too much. And they had disturbed my sleep. Hara-kiri. I decided to twist it.

"I have a question Sir."

"Yeah. Sure. Glad to answer. And don't call us Sir. I am Abhay and he is Sulabh." Sulabh was the I-schol.

"How does it feel being at McKinsey. Is it as great as you try to make it out? Did you really want to do this when you were on campus. Did you really imagine this ever since you were a kid?"

I could sense that I had stirred a forgotten corner in their heart. Sulabh shuffled uneasily but kept control. He twitched his fingers as if an unsolvable equation had been tossed at him. Abhay looked more shaken. He moved his fingers over the t-shirt. "It's lonely at the top."

"You have made me reflective, Romal." He eased into the chair.

The silence resonated with our words.

"You know, you are right. I sometimes wonder if this is what I wanted. Many a times I have questioned it. I never found an answer, to be honest. Now I have just stopped asking." He pressed his face between his palms. Did I just hear a soft whimper?

Sulabh pressed his shoulder to comfort him. I sensed melodrama. But then I am melodramatic. I would have liked Abhay to take out a hanky and wipe his moist eyes. No such luck. His eyes were not moist enough.

Abhay appeared to have gotten lost in his own world. I didn't expect him to be so fragile that a small unexpected stroke would rattle him so much. I didn't know what to feel for him. Sorry? Sympathetic? Condescending? Sulabh moved towards my balcony. He looked towards the blue sky which was turning grey. Clouds on the horizon matched the gloomy mood inside. Evening lights had appeared. The world outside went on as normal. I could hear the chatter of evening joggers and walkers. There were some tempo-shouts between various dorms. They were putting their rhyming skills to good use by forming and hurling abusive couplets at each other. Somewhere within the campus there would be people worrying about tomorrow's class, yesterday's quiz, today's results. Somewhere romance may be blossoming; somewhere it could be giving way to its ultimate breakup. I could see so many of my brethren busy with so many things I had done in so many days of stay on campus. Studying, playing, worrying, arguing, tea-ing, planning, partying, eating, sleeping, pissing… But I could see none doing what I was doing right now. Making two stalwarts from McKinsey cry. Making them reflective. Bringing them in touch with their own forgotten self. Fucking their happiness, basically. Ah! Such a pleasure. But I couldn't show it. Not yet. I had to wait till they leave. But they were not to without handing me a return gift.

"Romal, you are blessed. For you are asking questions at the right time. This is the time," spoke Sulabh. His face sincere, showing deep reflection. Strangely, his sincere concern scared me. I have often been the victim of well intentioned advice. It has never worked. I told you earlier how IIMA has an exchange program. I had a chance at it. I could have gone to Paris. On full scholarship, for I was an I-schol. In the land of hot, long-legged, brunette who dole it out to whosoever wants. I am not kidding. That is what one of our dorm tuchcha told us. He had returned from there. But he didn't want it. Even if that was folklore, I wanted to believe in it. Like Mr Harivansh Rai Bachchan has stated, 'Pleasure is not so much in getting what you want but in lusting for it'. But I chose not to go. For a tribunal of three of our beloved tuchchas advised Suman and me that given our good performance and bad history, it would be advisable to stay back and earn CV points by participating in contests. That shall bolster our chances in the final placement. We followed their advice, but partially.

We stayed back but forgot everything else. I didn't know how to stop Sulabh from what he was about to do. I hadn't yet learned how to handle such situations. I have learned now. One should run away from intelligent, wise, experienced people. You never know what's on their mind. You can't trust them. They will listen to your story feigning all the sincerity while in their mind they may be designing their own agenda. To trap the free spirits and turn them into themselves, slaves. To know your story and learn from it. That is what they want really. They would go to any length for learning I tell you. No use is this learning and all I tell you. Yeah, I am telling you right. I don't normally do that. Tell the truth, I mean. But this time it is. Hundred percent, unadulterated, truth. Hey, don't run away from me now!!

What followed was a long, tiring, exhausting and all encompassing discussion for over two hours. Leave the details and just know the outcome. It's worth it. It screwed my happiness for the rest of the year and sometimes I feel it is still sticking up my arse like the tail-bone. Long extinguished but remains still lingering. Of no use but a potential trouble maker. He handed me two models to structure my thoughts to get better mental clarity about what I want or rather what I shall want. Below is the visual representation of the two frameworks.

a) Understanding what all you want through sliced circle framework (Hidden agenda: Designed to convert you into split personality)

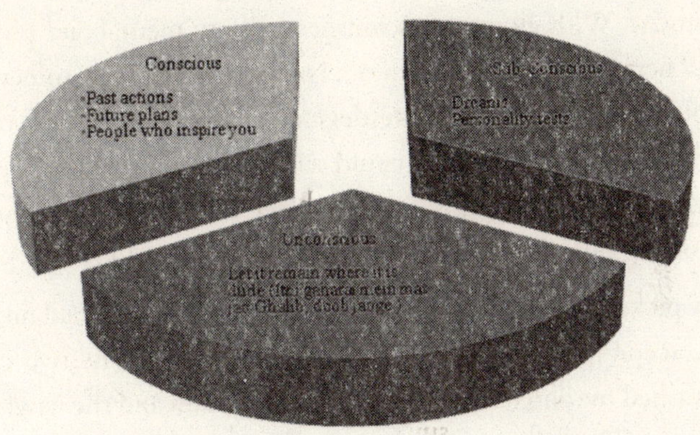

It provides techniques for finding out what you want. Work along each slice and see yourself developing like a full circle.

b) Understanding why you want what you want through concentric circles framework (Hidden agenda: Designed to make you go round and round)

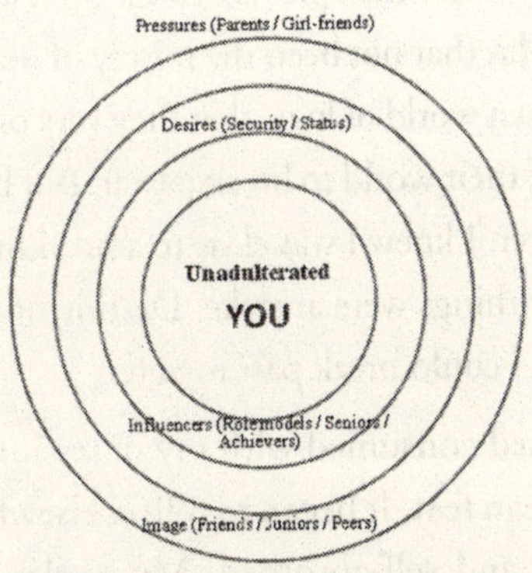

It requires you to associate what you want with reasons for it. As you would reach closer to the centre, you would be reaching to the centre of your existence; that is you.

I was in one of those rare moods. Of being completely present in the moment. With all my consciousness, all my mental and physical energy. There was no buzz in my head. No thoughts of being somewhere else, doing something else. No restlessness, no anxiety. I began to feel grateful towards the duo. They could sense it and it lifted their spirits. What they couldn't do for themselves, they could help someone else with. Sorting oneself out. To the last level of thought.

They picked up their hats and moved away. Okay, they had no hats. But the scene looked directly out of Men in Black. The two came, brain-washed me and left. I jumped on to my notes and the newfound frameworks. They were my map to myself!

The next few days were very tense as I began to introspect and ask hard questions. Slowly I began to move towards the centre of my existence. The central point of my being, the reason for my existence was about to be revealed. I could sense it but couldn't capture it. My rational mind prevented me from reaching out to the real me. Beyond the reach of normal thought, beyond everything that human kind has ever witnessed. Reason is a device of mind which prevents itself from following itself. I was so close. Yet so far. Has that not been the misery of mankind? Trapped so much within their own world of logic that they very often find themselves scratching the pits of their world to break past it. But how often have they been successful? Never. I knew I was close to a breakthrough. It was more than just me. Larger things were at stake. Destiny of the mankind could be altered. If, if only I could break past myself.

A few weeks passed consumed with my obsession with getting past myself. It was no mean feat. It began to reflect elsewhere. I had become irritable, stubborn, and self-absorbed. My grades dropped. I began to miss submissions. I couldn't care less about anything. I continued running. I kept thinking. I had to physically tire myself to sleep. The question hounded me even in my dreams. One day as I ran, Jhaadu tried to play with me. He blocked my way and attempted preventing me from running. His girl-friend, Polly stood by, amused. I warned Jhaadu not to do that. But he was even more amused. My resistance egged him on. That day I had a feeling that today could be the day of the breakthrough. I had been having omens since morning. That morning, on an impulse I went to my balcony. I hardly ever used to stand in my balcony. That day I did. I didn't know why. The moment I did, I knew why. The dorm adjacent was a girl dorm. One of the girls was changing her dress. I became a witness to that. On some other occasion I would have reacted differently but I was on the mission to save the mankind. I knew there is more to it than meets the eye. It was an omen. It was the signal that I was waiting for. I was inching towards breaking past my rationality. I warned Jhaadu one last time. I implored Polly, his girlfriend. She found the game funny. I was irked. As I ran my lap, Jhaadu followed and jumped in front of me. I kicked him in his balls. He fell on the ground. Polly ran towards him. After all, her favourite part of Jhaadu had been hit. What will he be without them? What will she do with him without them? Jhaadu, if you happen to read it, pardon me, for now you know my reasons for taking such an extreme step. You were coming in the way of altering mankind's destiny. Small sacrifice, I say.

I was deeply disturbed that night. Due to Jhaadu's childishness, I had probably lost my chance. Nothing worked. I was inconsolable. It was Friday night. One of the usual ramp parties were on. I went for that. I ran into Choku there. Choku was a stud. He had dared to spurn the I-banking offer. He was rarest of the rare. He had interned with one of the I-Banks and got final offer too. Life could be sex, booze and party for him. But he had decided not to accept the offer. He hadn't finalized what he wanted to do. "But not that banking shit," were his now famous words. "I don't want to live by the clock. I am a free man. I shall live and die like one," he had said. He was a poor man too. And chances were he would live and die one as well. As one sows, so one reaps. He had decided not to sow anything so he would not have the headache of reaping. Damn smart, I say. He was closest to being irrational I knew. His long shoulder length tresses flowing in the wind, beads around his neck, he looked everything I wished to be. Minus his stinking body I mean. Suddenly there was another omen. Choku was pitch drunk. He was running around in circles. Big circle. Small circle. Concentric circles. I had begun to get used to omens now. I didn't react. Getting hold of him I took him to a corner. He looked directly in the eye. A connection was established. Enlightenment was evident from his face. He could see the seed of the same in me.

"What is it?" he asked. His hand on my shoulder.

"How did you get those long hair? I want them too. But all I get is shower drainage full of them," I stammered placing my deserting hairs into some shape.

"I faced that problem too."

I looked on silently. My quizzing eyes burning on his face.

"Drainage pipe used to get choked regularly. That's how I got named Choku." He let go of a cigarette puff.

"I decided to stop bathing altogether." Winners don't do different things, they do things differently. Studs don't do things altogether.

"But that couldn't be your real problem. With a face like yours, long hair would have done little good. A good seat can't run a broken scooter." Besides being a visionary he could see like ordinary men too. Reverence dripped from me. I shared my problem with him. He understood. Only he could have. Soon both of us were running in concentric circles. He in the bigger one and I in the smaller one. We swapped circles. We stood on the opposite end of the diameter of the largest circle and ran towards the centre. Our heads collapsed. Everything came out. But breakthrough was still far. We decided to try shock therapy. He lit a cigarette. I extinguished it on my left hand. No result. Fucking strong it is, this rationality. It was past 11:00 pm. We lay exhausted in the LKP field. LKP was designed for the students of IIMA to be able to run in largest possible concentric circles. Though no one has been able to discover this facet of it yet.

I wanted to give up. "Fuck off", I shouted watching towards the sky.

"You know Romal why I gave up that I-Banking offer?" suddenly Choku asked in a sentimental voice.

"Why? Because you wanted to do what your heart desires."

"Huh! You also fell for that shit. I just cooked that up. The real reason is that I was sorely disappointed when I came to know the IPO process."

I silently heard. These were words from Messiah.

"Like Martin Luthar King, I too have a dream. Ever since I got internship with the I-Bank, my dream was that when I would conduct the IPO, I would gather all potential investors in a large field. Then I would choose the best models from India. I would design special tees for them. The shares would be stuck to the back of their tees. A game of 'catch and run' would be played. Catch the model and tear the share document from the back of her tee and the share is yours. You know it has many potential benefits."

"Like?" I was deeply impressed. He was a visionary.

"Investors would be physically healthy. It is important. Process would be transparent. Everything will happen in the open. But I was told it is not legally permissible. So I quit."

Closing our eyes we absorbed the silence, silently praying for the idea to come true. For the greater good of the mankind.

"Let us go. I know what you need," Choku said getting up. I

followed.

We entered Choku's messed up room. He began to make a few calls.

"Okay, what about the other one? No, not Reshma, the previous one?" he enquired, continuing, "ya..ya...that one...theek hai, send her. Will pay you tomorrow."

Placing the phone down, he opened the table drawer and brought out a pudiya of grass. He spread it on the table.

"Prepare it while I am away. Shall be back in a while."

I nodded.

"And separate the seed," he said moving out.

"Why?"

"It will make you impotent," he shouted from outside. As if potency is being put to any good use.

He came back with his neighbor Khisko. Khisko held a whiskey bottle. Choku played hard metal. It grew on me. I wanted to drown myself in the noise. A little while later, there was a loud thud on the door. Opening the door Khisko whistled. A Nepali girl walked in. Wearing a t-shirt and jeans, she looked like a college student. She was accompanied by an older woman. Couple of rounds of drinks and joints ensued. I found it funny, drinking with prostitutes. *At least there is something common between Manto and I. Sadat Hassan Manto, I mean. All that I need is to begin writing to justify my actions.* Khisko held the older looking woman by the hand and dragged to his room. I let my hands slip under the tee of the Nepali girl. Khisko returned in a while, followed by the older woman.

Choku looked at me and gestured. I got up. The Nepali girl followed me to the Khisko's room. She sat on the bed consciously. A little light from the streetlamp was filtering in through the glass window. I stood at some distance from the bed looking at her. I didn't quite know what to do. Manto had never written beyond this point in enough detail. I closed my eyes for a moment. A strange mix of emotions were churning inside. Pity for her. Pity for myself. And a lot of turbulence underneath. There was a tussle between the poet and the beast. I didn't intervene. I didn't care about them anymore. I had decided to overlook them long back. Soon I could sense the beast taking charge. It had broken off its ropes and was roaming freely within me. Its eyes glared, tongue hung down wet with saliva and canine teeth bared. It roared and jumped forward. Moving closer to the bed took off my shirt and vest. Touched her cheeks. Encouraged, she moved her hand on my chest and stomach. I took off the rest of me. Holding her shoulders I pushed her back. She lay on the bed. I threw myself on top of her. My weight was still on my elbows as I straightened her legs with mine. I found her lips and kissed. There was little resistance. There was nothing of anything. I felt I am sucking a tree. Asked her to treat me like her lover. She looked with strange, confused eyes. It was an unusual request probably. She was too used to being used. She was not used to meeting future Mantos. I thought if she knows we are from IIMA and provides student discount. I didn't anyway. I took off her t-shirt. She unhooked her bra as I fumbled with them. I took her hand to places I wanted her to touch. Took my body portions closer to her lips. She began to understand me a little now. "You have very strong shoulders," she apprised me. "Hmmm..." I grunted as I continued chewing her breasts. I palmed one of them and pushed my teeth into her neck. Took out the rest of her clothes. She had begun to shake a bit. My movements had become violent. In that moment, in that act of bodies, I had forgotten my mind, myself. All of me was moving at the same time. Left hand, right hand. Left leg, right leg. Chin, lips. Chest, hips. All at the same time. All on their own. After long they were free. There was no one commanding them, telling them what to do. My mind didn't exist. I didn't exist. I was left to being just a set of discreet organs, loosely joint by outside skin and inside bones. Letting go of a moan she tried to hold me with her hands. My hair came in her fists. She tugged at them. I gave a wolf cry and continued. Was rubbing myself against her body. I travelled down. Something held me as I reached near her navel. I looked up. It was my cross locket. It had gotten entangled with her locket to form a bond. From the middle of this bond hung Jesus Christ! I couldn't look over it. I couldn't betray Jesus Christ. The poor guy had already been betrayed by so many. I didn't want to add to his misery. Wolf gave a shrill cry. It knew it is about to lose its control. It gave one more try. It threw itself over her and sucked. It didn't help. Something had dried inside. I felt like a tree. Stiff and numb. The wolf retreated. Back to its cage. The mind came back. The organs rejoined. They were aching at the joints. They didn't look too happy to be back in each other's company. In the greater good of God's son I stepped down. She looked surprised at my actions. Wearing her clothes she came upto me and touched my cheek. I could see semblance of love in her eyes. I smirked at myself. *Place you go for sex offers you love. Those you go for love, offer you sex. Loser with a big L you are, I tell you.* Self pity took me over as I moved out. Choku stopped us in the way and took the Nepali girl back to Khisko's room. Loud noises emanated from the room. The older woman was gulping drinks and shouting. "He is a Rakshas. His wife would die of pain." "Let us do it again. No money this time." She threw herself over Khisko. We all have a beast within us. No matter what we look on the outside. What we see is just the pretence of education coated social conditioning. Scrape it out and we are back to our origins. Beasts. 'We are not what we show, we are what we hide,' so I believe. We do not learn how to tame the beast as we get educated. We learn how to camouflage it. We learn how to hide our real human nature behind the garb of nice sounding words, cover it with layers. We do not remain 'we' any more. We become the idea of how we shall be. We become marketeers of ourselves, we become image creators, we become rationalizers. Quickly suppressing under the carpet the part of us that we are, which we have been but which we would much rather not present to anyone. We learn so many things but we never really forget who we are or what we should not be. A deep sense of nausea came over me. Feeling suffocated I moved out. I went into the bathroom. My skin was itching near the cheeks, near the chin, on the chest, back, everywhere. Everywhere she had touched. I took off my clothes, brushed my teeth repeatedly and gargled. I kept rubbing myself with water. There was a bang on the door. It was Choku.

"What are you doing? Been long…"

"Will be back in a sec…"

It would take long. It would take a longer time to clean myself than I have tonight. As the beast had begun to subside, the me that I sometimes am had begun to reclaim me. Making me aware more than ever that I am not them. I am not Choku. I am not Khisko. The self-assured beasts. The self-realized humans. *I don't know who I am but I am not them. I have a beast like them. But I also have a poet and a philosopher on my side. They are not letting me be like others. Impulsive and desirous. Susceptible to human weaknesses and follies. They are filling me with guilt and shame by rubbing me from within. I can't get rid of them. They are part of me. And I can't live with them.* Damn hard they are I tell you. This tug of the many me was killing me. I fell on the ground and prayed to Jesus Christ. "I have shown you respect, you have to show some mercy. Do something for me," I mumbled. There was no lightening, no thunderstorms but I felt as if something is being written on the sky. "It is your purpose in life," said a voice in my head. I didn't look up. I wasn't interested in knowing it anymore. I felt something flash in my head. I didn't pay heed. *I don't want to know myself anymore. I just want to be. In peace and beyond.* Even Jesus Christ had got me wrong. Like everyone else. *There is no hope for me, in this world and beyond.*

Personal confession: *Kaise kahoon.* I am embarrassed like Renuka Shahane was in the first sanitary napkin ad of India. I know you are disappointed with my action of not taking note of the message of the Jesus Christ. I totally agree with you there. I often feel angry with myself for doing so. Not for the personal loss I may have incurred by losing the chance at finding my sole purpose but the greater loss of…well… humanity. Moslems say that the Prophet was the last messenger after Jesus. Jews are still waiting. For their last prophet I mean. Well, for all you know, I could have been that Prophet everyone is waiting for. Hindus also talk about this prophet thing. Just that they are waiting for Kalki so am out of contention for sure just on the gender basis. Thank God for small mercies. What if Jesus' message was that you are the next prophet in line. Go save the world. What would I have done? Where would I have gone? It's just way too much responsibility you see. I wasn't ready for it. I still am not. I felt scared then. Also, I wasn't in my senses. What with the previous night me being doped and all. So much so that the whole night with Choku is blurry in my headspace. Am not saying so to cover up my actions as fiction. No I really did them. I have proof of it but won't tell you. It's not a gentlemanly thing to kiss and tell. We had a pact that night. Not Choku and me. Like hell I care for him anymore. He is no more a stud. Last he was spotted near the Jaipur highway. Must still be telling his "not that banking shit" story to those who care to listen. I don't. It was me and the Nepali girl who had it. Had the pact I mean. To not talk about it. I have reneged I know. But that is just to keep the story authentic. So much am suffering for it. And for your pleasure, dear reader. But it still is true what I tell you. No, not that I have a proof. When will you ever guess me right man. That I was quite dopey that night. But I would give out another truth as bargain. I gave the credit for giving me the two models to arrive at my reason of existence to the McKinsey people. That is not true. They are of really no good use. The Mckinsey and all I mean. You can test the model on yourself and let me know the results. Just curious, just like that. No hidden agenda and all I tell you. Seriously, no kidding. I am not like those wise and experienced people I keep bashing. I am a straight forward simple chap. I am. I really am. A dope head, I mean. Not always but often. I was that night. I was a dope head that night, I mean.

No remains of the last night were visible the next day. Khisko had left and Choku lay asleep on the floor, in a pool of vomit. He got up as I opened the door.

"Where are you going?" he asked.

"To freshen up."

"Wake me once you are done. Let's go for tea."

I tried to trace some memory of last night on his face but was disappointed. I got into the bathroom, under the shower. I could feel my body still itching. As if something is stuck to it. Some kind of dirt, some invisible object. It was not getting washed away with water. My clothes from last night lay in a heap. I put them in a polythene and went out.

I kept walking along the road till the heat began to burn my skin and feet began to wobble. I found a dustbin nearby and dumped the polythene into it. A few urchins were eyeing me. They were probably waiting for me to leave so that they can check the contents of the packet for some food or valuable. I wanted to discard more. I looked at my hands. I wanted to scratch out my skin and dump it too. But I couldn't. I was helpless. I am often a coward. I was one at that moment. I took out the cross and left it over the packet. It had done its job. I felt weak. I wanted to reach home before I fainted. I called out for an auto. I could see the kids trying out my clothes. One of them wore the cross-locket. It dangled against his bare chest. The locket knew whom it shall belong to.

Reaching the room, I collapsed on the chair. I checked mails. A dozen companies to be applied to. Many a forms to be filled. There was no running away from them. Not knowing my purpose meant one would be imposed upon me. "Why did I become so emotional and not take note of the purpose?" I chided myself. Emotions never pay in retrospect. But they are still preferable for sanity just never pays. A tiny paper slipped out from under my desktop keypad. I pulled it out. The handwriting appeared to be mine and all but it was too zagged to be sure. Below is what I found:

Settle the original dispute of the world
between monkeys & orangutans
Who gets to live on mango tree & who
gets the banana?

Personal confession: I know. I know. After all the search and chagrin what did I get? Monkey and Orangutan! Think of my trauma. But it was no trauma really. It was quite a lift. My shoulders slumped as after a heavy stone being lifted off them. I was born 5000 years too late. The purpose of my life had already been solved by nature. I was left to live free, as per my wishes. I love you Jesus.

No really. I meant it. I didn't say it like Rakhi does. Rakhi Sawant I mean. And Prophet Mohammed (PBUH) and Kalki too. I love them too I mean.

15
PLACEMENTS: KILL ME SLOWLY, OH NO!

Angels, Demons, and I: The meeting, in a dream or somewhere in the sky, I don't know

I had a strange dream. I always do but this one was special. I remember it very vividly. I sat in a board room with a large centre table, a projector screen hung nowhere. Walls were not visible, nor was the floor. It looked like a room located nowhere. Two sets of people sat on the either side of the table. The first set had a halo ring over them. Like they say angels have. The elderly one was a portly, middle-aged man. His face looked kind, considerate, and experienced. It had a hint of mischief too. He looked like someone who has witnessed many weather storms and has a responsible job. He probably didn't like certain parts of his work, I thought. His pock-marked face was kind of ugly. But he had a grace. His hand kept going to his untidy beard. He wore a cross. His jacket also bore the symbol. Next to him sat a young guy of age similar to mine. He was looking as if he knew me very well. I am not sure if I knew him. He could be someone from that farm party I had been to months back. I had gotten drunk and danced with a beer bottle on my head. Before It fell and hurt someone's face. 'Was he that fellow and am I in some kind of court?' I guessed. I threw a smile at him. *Might help me escape easily.* It was my backup plan. I always have one.

The man on the other side looked more intelligent than his counterpart. He had sharp features, an aquiline nose and looked quite fit for his age. His peculiar eyes, had a tinge of green and brown. The colours kept changing. He looked manipulative and mean. I wouldn't normally do business with him. He had a strange tail he kept flapping on the table. Like demons have. It appeared to be coming out of his arse. I was amused. He wasn't at my response. Amused I mean. He flapped it. The tail I mean. The young man standing behind him looked disgusting. Not literally. He was slightly fat and had a double chin. He wore a shirt and a tie. He had a smaller tail, not long enough to reach the table though he did wag it. *Is it a juvenile court or something? Too much of costume drama for breaking a beer bottle in a party I say. Naah, it has to be a dream. Been long I had a good one. They must have thought to dress up like clowns to engage me.*

I was thrilled with the whole thing. I never had had this kinda dream before. Looked like a break from my boring routine. A book on dreams I had read said that our intuition is sharpened during dreams and they can foretell our future. I took a mental note of everything. It may throw up something I wouldn't want to miss.

The two gentlemen looked at each other. One with the tail took the lead. He squirmed in his suit. It had '666' inscribed over it. A thought came and I shivered. I parked it to let the proceedings tell me where I am.

The one with the tail: "Okay. So Romal, see it's a very uncommon situation. Let me introduce ourselves. I am Project Manager, demons division. I look after over 16008 people primarily in the western India region. Yeah, the place you are located in."

The portly man: "Ahem. We can curtail the details. Let's come to the point."

The one with the tail: "Hmm. Romal, we have a proposal. Listen very carefully for we only have five minutes for this meeting. And you have no idea how much of work has gone in arranging this..."

The portly man: "Ahem. Proposal please."

The one with the tail: "Yeah. So, we have a deal. You need to choose and tell us your preference. What you say will determine your future or certain events in it. Are you ready?"

The portly man got up. Walking across he put his hands on my shoulders. I experienced a kind of cold energy flowing through me. "Romal, we know the situation you are in. You like this girl but she doesn't like you. Right?" He sat next to me looking into my eyes. My dismay was evident as I had never let it out.

"Don't look so surprised son. Okay, we are angels and demons. Yeah, we do exist. In some way we are responsible for some of the situations you find yourself in. And we want to do something about it."

The one with the tail: "And we have for you a choice, between that love of yours and the Day-0 job. You make a choice and we get it for you, just like that. What do you want?"

'To become the President of USA,' I wanted to say. It was my childhood ambition. It looked like the right forum for such wishes. But that was not on the menu. Alas! I couldn't make myself say it aloud so I secretly thought of it, hoping they would read it, them being angels and all. That would have solved all my problems. Instead of being at the mercy of Day-0 company interviewers, I would be deciding their fate in their own land. And even Varsha won't be able to resist the charms of Mr President of US of A. Such a neat plan I say. Such a clever guy I am. I know. I know. Don't you smile. I know.

The portly man: "And I need to tell you something more. We have control over the Day-0 thing. If we say so, we can do so. But this other thing, we can try but well, there is no guarantee."

"What do you pick?" the two said together.

Huh! There goes my chance at becoming Mr President. Some things about me even angels don't understand. Anyway, let us come back to the glum plum reality. Back to the dough and water, the usual grind. Okay, guys, just stay quiet. Time to introspect. I closed my eyes. Varsha's face swirled. Everything else blanked out. She was my only star in the cloudy dark night. I want to use a better allegory but I don't have one. My writing prowess cannot match the strength of her grip over me. *If I have a chance? If I truly have a chance? This is stupid. I must be dreaming. Oh, my God. I still haven't been able to get over her. Have I? But still...*

I opened my eyes. "I choose her." Just like that. Melodrama, you say? Yeah, kind of. But it's okay mate. I like melodrama. Life gives you Hollywood; you make Bollywood out of it. I like Bollywood movies. They are...anyway. Cut the crap. More on that later. You keep making a list of things I have promised to tell later. Okay, mate?

"Are you stupid? There is no guarantee of that. Why not take what we want to offer," the one with the tail screamed.

I stood silent.

"You deserve what you are getting you...you..."

The portly man stood smiling. He had been a human once. This is what he liked about his job. Witnessing human folly. This irrationality. He had long since become incapable of it.

The placements were to start the next day. I sat on the chair, feet on either side of the computer. A nude girl prompted on screen, "Hi

Romal" It wasn't a fantasy. There is a software like that. Go, check it. Did you say, sick? Haan? Sorry, be louder. I can't hear you properly. Anyway, it is not about you. It is about me. You can go and fuck yourself. Sorry for that. But am trying to meditate. More on that later. Put that in the list I asked you to create earlier. What? You forgot about it! Huh. Now I am going to forget about all that too. Game equal. Shut up now. Tomorrow was full of uncertainty. I could hear muffled voices outside. Others were nervous too. Everyone was. In a day life could change like anything. We all came here with different levels of dreams. Some knew what they were getting into and what for. Most didn't. I didn't. I-bank, consult, big jobs, dollar salary etc. etc., whatever whatever. For good or bad, it had become our dream. Media and people around us made sure it becomes. The average salary of an IIMA grad was public knowledge. If you go and tell them the reality, people may not even believe you. Loser, they would quickly label you. And then there always was this next question, "If not this, then what? Entrepreneurship? Needs capital. Do you have it? And what about the risk? Do you think you have it in you?" Self doubt is the bane of intelligence. We may always be questioning if this is the thing we wanted or was it just the popular culture. But we hardly ever questioned our ability to say 'No' to it. We knew that we didn't have it. We kept trying to accept or find reasons to make it look like our own choice. *May be I can do it for two years. Can earn money and come back. Dad needs the money*, was my reason. *What if...* came second thought. I felt scared. Thoughts of failure are too scary. Especially the ones which you don't understand. I gulped water. *Is there a way out? I really don't want these jobs. I really don't want to go.*

On the floor below, Jhaadu sat on his balcony wall, smoking leisurely. Polly stood nearby, her hand rubbing his balls. 'They must still be hurting from my kick,' I smirked. Jhaadu used to get only about five puffs per cigarette, rest of the cigarette got burned in ferrying between 'smoking hand on the thigh position' and lips. I scanned through the girls' dorm. No further omens today. Guys in the dorm in front of ours' were wandering semi-dressed. One of them, Leaky, clad in a loose white vest hurled abusive epithets. I didn't respond, gave a meek smile instead. They didn't like it. Leaky along with a few others came below our dorm and began to piss.

"What are you all doing?" Jhaadu called out. Placing her hands on her mouth Polly said, "awww." I wasn't sure what was it for. For their act or for what was doing the act. I didn't want to know. There was activity in couple of girls' rooms. None of it looked interesting. I felt dissociated from my usual banality. After wetting our dorm walls, Leaky and his associates had begun to march back. "Dorm barah ke bachche, chhakke chhakke," they shouted. Couple of dorm mates had come out in their balcony. They tried to counter but were no match. They called upon me to join. I struggled with myself. I decided to join in. "Dorm nine walon ka jitna lamba hai, usse wo kar sakate keval geela khamba hain," I hurled back. Leaky brigade left. My gauntlets returned. Life had taken away my jigsaw puzzle and handed me a riddle. I decided to go for a jog. Jogging always made me feel better. For I would be doing something without really doing something.

Evening was pleasant. Ground was green. But I couldn't enjoy myself. Placement worries had covered me like a smog. Long term thinking puts a strain on the inevitable today. I took a deep breath and let go of tomorrow from my mind. I felt relaxed.

Slowly they emerged. The others. They began to jog along. Poet on my side, philosopher walking behind briskly, beast moving back and forth impatiently, racing ahead then waiting for us to catch up. Master appearing at a distance and then disappearing.

"Romal, what have you thought of the placements?" asked the poet. "You should make the right choice now," he continued. I wished them to be silent.

"You should try social venture or something. Do something for the society," he suggested. I grunted.

"Or may be something academic Romal, like a Ph. D," suggested the philosopher, his face aglow with a soft wish. I wanted someone to throw cold water over him.

"Noo…not Ph. D. So boring and so long," the beast barged in. I did love him sometimes. "Why not advertising? They have the best girls," he said licking the ground.

The harmony had been strained with their differing suggestions. Perturbed, I looked ahead. Varsha was coming from a distance. I brightened up. I knew what I wanted. I wanted her. She was a wish. She had no reason. She just was. Beyond her, there were no wish. There were choices. Thoughts about the dream I had, with angels and demons, revisited. I wondered if it was true. I wanted it to be. Without it the wish was to go unfulfilled. I looked up at the sky. I wanted Him to hand me my wish or to take away His choices. I didn't want a choice. I just wanted. My mobile rang. *Has God started direct line?* I picked it up. Mobile I mean. It was from my friend back home. God still operated in ways of 5,000 BC. I silently heard the news. I sank further. Dad had had a heart attack. His business partner had made fraud allegations against him. He had been in police custody for the last couple of days. My home could get mortgaged. He couldn't take it. I could. I could see God's hand in it. It has to be. He has always been on my side. It couldn't be otherwise. God had shown me the way. He always does. I unnecessarily crib about Him all the time. It was his way of enabling me to make a choice. He delivers even with obsolete technology. Technology is just another choice for him. Like everything else.

Everyday is a new day. Everyday is a new fight. I wanted to believe in it. I hadn't read *Gone with the Wind*. I didn't know *Scarlett O'Hara* and the famous line, *tomorrow is another day*. But I was trying to live that. I deserve at least fifty points for this fight without inspiration. The purpose of placement was becoming unclear. *Even if I get somewhere, would I want to go? Would I be able to go? Should I chuck it all? Will I be able to take the burden of this decision?* The problem with dilemma is that it multiplies. You solve two, it comes back with four. You just need to break past it. I decided to do what I always do. I wait till the last minute to take the jump. I give time a chance to give me another chance. I donned a black suit and red tie, picked up my folder with documents. No interviewer would ever ask for them but it looks neat. It is a part of the warrior's armour. Some for protection, some for style. Who would really like to go to war if there is no glory associated with it? Fake or real. Remember *Troy*? Brad Pitt said in it that there is no glory in death. No matter where it comes. In the battle ground or in a paddy field while shitting, it's the same. But by the time you know the truth it's too late. And who would listen to you even if one tries to tell. Like in all these big glamorous jobs. By the time you realize that the glorious part of it is left outside the chamber where you slog like an ass, it is too late. You should go to war if you love to fight. Love the contest. Go to these jobs if you love the money. Love the analysis. Not because you will get to fly in a plane and live in five star hotels. Never. Anyway, enough *gyaan*. Why care about those who don't care about anyone else. The point is I was nervous, or rather there was no point actually to anything that I was doing. I was just doing. It didn't matter what I did. Why I do anything if it doesn't matter anyway? I am still to find an answer to that. I am still doing.

I had been shortlisted by more than ten companies. I was an I-schol. Interviews began. Consulting companies were the first. They threw me out in the first round. One of them showing mercy took me to second round and then threw out. It felt the same. Next day it was time for the banks to slaughter me. I kept getting in and out of them. They kept asking the same questions. Why banking? Which side of banking? Tell me something about yourself. I kept trying new versions of the answer.

Why banking?

1. What else is there to do?
2. When I look at you, I feel I want to be you.
3. I am not sure. Why don't you tell me?

Which side of banking?

1. Trading. I am good at quick math.
2. Investment banking. I love stock markets.
3. I will let you decide it for me. I am raw talent. You hone me.

It didn't matter what I said, result was always the same. I tried counting my pile of bad luck. Easy. As many interviews, as many exits. All first rounds. Life sucks. I am an idiot. Is there a better word? Sorry, worse word. Whatever. I felt pathetic. I looked up. There were two kinds of people around, happy and not bothered. Oh, there was one more kind. Mine. I wanted to go. Run away. Where to? Not that there was a place good enough. I closed myself in a room. This was the best I could think of. But there was still the Lehmann channel to be crossed.

Let's go, there is no use making yourself go through the ordeal, I told to myself.

No. I would not let you go till you finish. I don't want to hear tomorrow that I had a chance if only I would have gone in. They were looking for someone just like me or whatever. This was the fighter in me talking.

Idiot. I hated me.

"Romal," the person attending Lehmann Brothers called as I pulled myself up, straightened my suit and began to walk in the direction of the Lehmann room of course. The fighter always wins. At least with oneself.

The Lehmann guy had walked outside the room to welcome. Placing his hand on my shoulder he said, "Do we have that scary a reputation? You look as if we are gonna fry you inside." I let the barb go. Sorry. It was supposed to be funny. I was hardly in a mood to see the funny side.

There were two people inside. One looked directly out of some English movie. Name? Forget it. He was playing a professor in the movie. Nice, long, silky, well combed hair. Clean face. Eyes telling intelligence and desk work. Comfortable posture. Comfortable aura.

The other guy looked like a student of the professor. Thick glasses. Hands on the table, slightly bent. Eager for the next moment. Probably thinking about how to assess me. His eyes showed tremendous intelligence but of the mathematical kind. The frown in his eyes told that he had struggled to grapple with life outside mathematics.

I took my chair. Didn't wait for them to ask. As they didn't speak up immediately, I figured they were giving me time. I relaxed myself. Breathed in and exhaled. Of course I didn't let them notice this. I am not an idiot.

"So, Romal. I see. You are rank…20. I see, very impressive," the professor commented. "So, are you hoping to hear from any of the consult companies?" he continued. Results from consulting companies were already out. He was checking if I already have an offer which is an indicator of how desperate I would be. Also it was an indicator of how wanted I am.

"No, sir. I don't think so."

"Why, they suck or you suck?" It was the professor. So he had quite a tongue. That's why he was at Lehmann not at some University. Difference lies in attitude, not capability.

I pondered, well just a little. "Well sir, they think I suck and I think they suck," I stung back. Down, yes. Out? Not still.

"I like that. I like that. That's the attitude." The professor was almost jumping. Sorry, he didn't look like a professor anymore. At least I hadn't seen any like him. But don't count on my observation. I haven't seen many. And even among those I have, I hardly ever tried to notice them closely. Professors have this nasty habit of trying to teach you, trying to make you learn. And who wants to learn. Not me, at least. Anyway.

"So, which subject do you like the most?" Professor again.

This was the toughest question I had faced. I didn't like any. One has to study because one has to study. Period. But one has to answer too when a question is thrown at you.

"Mathematics sir, I think."

"Mathematics! That's great." Student this time. I was right. He lived on numbers. One...two...three...count and you are free.

"And what do you like in mathematics. I mean which part of it?"

I had heard that question before. In IIMK interview. I remembered what I had said then.

"Anything and everything."

"What do you mean by that? There must be something you like. You are just plain avoiding the question."

"No, I am not. You asked what do I like, I said all. There is no particular favourite. Its been years since I studied anything."

"Romal, I am only trying to help you here. I want to make it easy for you," the interviewer had said.

"I know sir. But frankly I don't have an answer. But you ask question. I am ready to try it and take full responsibility. If I fail, you can just plain chuck me out."

But that was then. It was now. I wanted to give a different answer. Creativity points if nothing else.

"Probability."

"Oh, great," student chuckled. Probability was his sweet dish.

First question. Something…something…

I tried answering. Something…nothing…nothing.

Next question. Same response.

"Romal would you like to try some other subject?"

"Macro economics," I said. I had great grades in it. But that was in the first year. Been a year since I had dealt with it.

"Sure." Different subject, same result. Something…something. Nothing…nothing.

Within a few minutes we knew that interview is going nowhere. But courtesy and culture is also something.

"So, Romal. Do you have some questions for us?"

Please, let me go, I said to myself.

No, ask question. Fighter again. This man I tell you.

"Does Lehmann have plans to enter India?" Fighter spoke. I died.

Professor weighed me. Culture. He had to answer.

He said something about there could be a plan but it is not clear and some more things. I was not hearing. He was just plain saying and wasn't really trying to tell me. What he wanted to tell, I wasn't listening.

"So, does that quench your query? Any…more questions."

"Yes, sir." Fighter. Fighter.

"Yess." He lost his comfortable posture and aura by now. The mathematician was uneasy and slightly sympathetic. His mind was calculating the probability of my asking five questions. His eyes were telling me to drop it. The professor was fidgeting.

I opened my mouth and immediately closed it. "Leave it sir. I guess we both know that it's over," I quickly said and began to pick up my certificate folder. They were taken aback by my sudden shift. They wanted to say something to cheer me up I guess. But the situation was larger than words. I left. Their eyes probably dropped me till outside the door. *But who would drop me till the door of my room?* No one. I dragged myself.

The scene from within my room was similar to the way it was within me. Dark inside and bright outside. Could hear the laughter of people. It was a celebration time for many. Foreign jobs, dollar earnings. *Not for me. Not for me. I am to India what Delhi Police is to its people. For you, with you, always.* I had no energy and motivation left for further interviews. There was no tomorrow. Whiles others appeared to have forgotten, my usual supporters came in. Out of their sense of duty I presumed.

"Romal..." came the familiar voice. I had already prepared my response. I stayed firm and cold. Beast came close and began to lick my feet. I kicked him in the gut. He flew back, hit the wall and recoiled. Horrified, others gathered around him.

"Romaal..." shouted the Master. Poet also was startled. Even philosopher was rattled.

"Go. Just go," I told them. I was livid.

"Romal, this isn't right!" poet protested. I stood with my back towards them. Master came forward and kept his hand on my shoulder. I shirked it down. Beast was still screeching in the background. Their presence was irritating. I hated their sympathetic tone.

"Romal, why are you being like this? We are your own," said the Master.

"I don't believe you all. No one is my own. Just leave. I feel special with you all around. I don't want to."

"But you are special," spoke the philosopher.

I wanted to stare down at them. I wanted to feel so incensed that I could break their heads. But I couldn't. All I could do was reason out. Nice substitute I say. "Well, then there are better ways to make me feel special then to make me go through this. If this is what being special is about, then thanks. Leave me to my ordinary self."

"Romal…" poet tried to intervene. I turned and folded my hands. "Please go," I said. They stood silent.

"Gooo," I shouted finding some energy back.

My stand was apparent. They found theirs and left. There was little left to be said.

As night grew, so did my desperation. I couldn't hold myself together. I didn't even know what was really hurting. It was just hurting. Keeping lights off, I sat on my chair, staring at the computer, as if hoping for something or someone to pop out of it. My eyes had turned bleary but I couldn't get myself to close them. The moment I did, many a thousand images would throng my mind, gripping me like a noose, suffocating me. I couldn't step out of my room. The outside world had no place for me anymore. There was hardly much left to get inside of myself. It was going to be a long night. I had little distance to travel.

Soon it began to get to me. I already had a history of heart attack in the family. I didn't want to start a trend there. I held my chest together and called up a school friend with whom I could feel self pity without really pitying myself. But he had turned into a jerk. He told me how I always do this. Tell the world I am fucked up before fucking them the next moment. I tried to convince him how I never really have fucked him but he didn't believe me. He was convinced that the reason he sometimes walks in an awkward way is me. I didn't know how to convince him otherwise. I hung up. It had left me nowhere. The conversation with the jerk I mean. It had made me thirsty instead. There was no water in the bottle and I couldn't make myself go outside. I thought of another prick who could help me. I called him up.

"Dodo, please help me," I said.

"Kya hua?"

"Nothing. Can you come to my room and take me somewhere. I am feeling very..."

"Ya, sure. I will just be there."

This Dodo was a great guy really. Great guys are not really useful. It is the useful guys who are great guys. Soon Dodo and I were out of the campus and on our way to dining place of a five star hotel. That is the best remedy to get me out of myself that Dodo could think of. Dodo liked to chew Rajanigandha and all. I hated it when he spoke with his mouth open. I wanted him to keep it shut. His mouth I mean. He was constantly telling me how it isn't end of the world. How there are more companies the next day, I can earn more money here also, life is a journey, etc. etc. Problem with useful guys is they are not really great. I just wanted someone to feel miserable on my behalf. I didn't have it in me to feel so myself. I was afraid the feeling might stay. I needed a conduit. I tried to create a situation which will make him feel so. Miserable for me, I mean. I told him my father was a rag picker and how I have struggled my way up to this place. Also that my mother had lung cancer and so it was really important for me to go abroad and earn money for her medicines and all. Dodo had grown on Govinda movies. Where in Govinda's mother stitches clothes but lives in a large house and Govinda wears Rayban glasses and ogles at Karishma Kapoor. Dodo's eyes immediately welled up. I began to feel better. Then I told him what had really been hurting. I told him that I actually believed that God had devised a plan in bringing me to this place. And after he made me an I-schol and all, I truly believed that he must have thought of a better exit plan than the one he had handed. Dodo became so choked on this one that he had to spit the Rajanigandha out. With a large portion of misery passing out of me via Dodo, I became capable of feeling something else. I felt hungry. As I got up and filled up my plate with desserts, Dodo came close and hugged. Looking at his crazy face, wet with tears, I couldn't stop myself from laughing. I could understand why he was named Dodo by his dorm-mates. It made Dodo feel even better.

After dinner he left me near my dorm. I couldn't say my thanks to him but I really was. Thankful I mean. I never say it when I really mean it. If I have ever said it to you then just know that I made an exception. Earlier I was trying to feel miserable but now I was. Feeling miserable I mean. I sneaked into my room and closed the door. Lying in the bed I knew I would be able to sleep in a bit. Some solace I say.

From now on, I wanted to make only promises that I could keep. I promised myself I will not appear for further placements. Tough choice I say. I had an offer from an IT company through lateral placement. *I will take it and leave it at that.* Lateral placements were for experienced folks and happened way before the final placements. But the fighter in me had other plans. It wanted to go and face the bull again. Another day, another fight. The optimist me. I had to erase the fighter before I could rest, I realized. Every bull needs a red flag. I was a dog, I needed a kick. All the time. Next day, I left my room door ajar. Secretly I was hoping that someone will come in. I knew no one would want to knock on my door knowing that I could be very fucked up. In America when someone is down and out they leave him to deal with it himself. I have nothing against America, it's a great country and culture and all but somehow I don't like this thing about them. I may be wrong about it for what did I know about it other than from the movies. And yeah, this thing about them I had picked from some movie only. Oh, it was an Hindi movie actually. Could be wrong then! So, where did these guys learn this thing? Anyway, the thing is the people who want to go to America need to first learn their culture and this part of their culture had been learned very well by my dorm mates. So they mostly stayed away. By afternoon, one of my juniors breached the code of American conduct and dropped into my room. There was little to be said. Moroseness was dripping out of me. He looked uncomfortable so I indicated that he may sit down on the same bed on which I was sitting. Big gesture I say!

"Dude."

I looked up a little.

"See, I know it's bad. But there are still a lot of good companies left."

I looked up some more.

"Merrill?" he said. He had got me wrong. It was not dearth of good companies that was hurting. It was hurt that was hurting.

"I have decided not to go for any more interviews. I am getting out of the system. I will pick up that IT job."

Silence. His uncomfortable gaze. My defiant look hung somewhere in the middle of the room.

"Look, you can do whatever you want to. Of course you are free to do so. But all I can say is that I will respect you more if you went for further interviews."

I didn't look up. But something had stirred in me.

"It had been a bad day. But don't give up on opportunities that may come tomorrow. It is just another day and will go by. But if you don't give it a fair chance you will regret it for long."

What was he doing? Going against American culture! Trying to pep me up! You just can't take India out of Indians. These bloody people!

"And I will be there during the process. But obviously you will have to go there." He left soon afterwards. Self respect takes you towards yourself. Respect of others beyond yourself. Useless travel I say.

Interviews became easy once the burden of expectations was off. I spoke freely. Tersely at times but not bitterly. I had applied only to a handful of companies on Day-1 so had only a few interviews to go through. Any company with a long form to be filled was dropped from my consideration set. '*I won't need to appear for Day-1 companies,*' I had reasoned. *And in case I would have to, I would hardly have any motivation left to take them anyway.* How well did I know myself! How little did I know my fate! How little did I understand life! I pretty much cleared all the interviews I had that day. But I had no selection criteria left. I was in the arms of destiny. Take me wherever you want. Just take me somewhere. Away from where I am. That is good enough. Merrill was the first one to make an offer. I accepted it and exited the placement process. It was an end. It was a beginning. I thought of the dream I had and the deal I had made with angels. *May be it is a part of that.* Another piece of reality filtered up. I keep viewing reality. I never become real. *I always get things once I have given up on them. I got through IIMA after*

I had stopped hoping for it. I became an I-schol once I began to not want it. I got the job after I had become indifferent. Maybe it is the same with Varsha. I will get her only after I have gotten over her. It didn't seem to be possible though. I didn't know what to wish for, to get her or to get over her? I didn't know what to feel. I wondered how should I be feeling, if I am a character in a fantastical story, with angels, demons, and all. *What does this event mean in the larger context of life about to come for someone fantastical like me.* Crazy motherfucker I was I say. A wry smile found its way despite myself as Varsha's face came in my mind. *Fuck yourself*, I said to the optimist in me and laughed out loudly. It wasn't really funny. But this was dramatic. I like drama. It was so damn insane. I like insanity. Sometimes. Once in a while. It was romantic. I like romance. Always. I am a little weird too. Didn't I tell you that earlier? But I didn't like it anymore. This weirdness. This need to see good in every situation. These alternative realities. *Where are they taking me? What will it look like when all of them converge? A summit of happiness and satisfaction or an abyss of no way out?* When the fountain of optimism and dreams dry, they leave you thirsty in scorching heat. Nothing can quench your thirst then. Nothing at all. I felt a burning sensation in my throat. I rubbed it a bit and let go of a sigh. I sat on the road pavement and watched the vehicles go. It was relaxing. To just be. Not do anything. Not expect anything. Just be a witness to time and meaningless events. I am a little weird. I like weird. Just a little bit. Anytime. Try it yourself. It's soothing. I thought of the others. I felt maybe I over reacted with them the other day. But I liked it this way. Away from them. It gave me peace. Maybe to them too. It was a win-win situation. Nice game, I won't say.

The convocation day had arrived. Everyone looked happy. For what reason, I wondered. For the life that had got over or for the one which was about to come. I couldn't see a reason to cheer in any. But I still had to. One must cheer when there are least reasons for it. I had gotten my degree from Mr. President. I must feel great. But it didn't. It was a big day. Looked like just another one. I missed my parents. I went to my room and remained there. This small room has been my house for two years. A bed flanked by an almira and a table. Whitewashed walls, fan with a thick layer of dust. A smile played on my lips. In two years I never found time to clean it. "Tomorrow!" I always said. Tomorrow never became today. It was time to move on. *I will miss you, my room. You may be shabby but you served me well.* People were coming. They wanted to wish me goodbye. I took it. I never say no to what life tries to bring. It may take away even that if I show *nakhara.*

"It is our last day dude. Let's make it count."

"Sure."

"I got hash. Brought it from Manali. Wanna try some?"

"Sure."

16
BACK TO THE PLATFORM

The train reached the station. It was a small station. That is why it was lovely. You know everything there including the tea vendors. I sat on the rickshaw.

"Ten rupees," he said.

"What? It's just five. I am not an outsider. I live in this city," I haggled. Just being there brings out the best in me.

"What *saahib*? I am not asking for too much."

"Come on, let's go. Take seven, okay. Nothing more. I don't earn. I am just a student." *IIMA hasn't changed me.* I smiled. I felt happy with myself. I placed my luggage on the seat and got onto the rickshaw.

Home always looks sweeter when you return after a long time. There is nothing special about it other than familiarity. With all, the good, the bad and the ugly. It's a small house. It's a small city. Dirty, crowded roads. Yes, people do chew *paan* and spit at inappropriate places. Actually they spit anywhere. There is no appropriate place for it. But it's still lovely. Friends may just barge into your home without calling you up and force you to come with them. "No," is not an acceptable answer. But I like it. This encroachment of privacy, of personal choice. As if they consider me to be no different than them. How badly had I missed them! I reached home. I gave the rickshaw puller ten rupees. It was never about money. It's about habit. It's about the small pleasures.

I directly went to my room. It looked the same the way I had left it. I spread myself on the bed. *Aah, it is so wonderful. I don't want to leave from here.* Ten minutes there and I began to itch. Familiarity is relaxing but it is boring. I liked adventure and action. A lot. I called up couple of friends. We fixed up to meet in a couple of hours. I got out of the room and looked for Ma. I was hungry. I needed food. That is how you remember the ones you love the most. You ignore any courtesy whatsoever. She was out somewhere but came in sometime. I waited for her eyes to find me and shine. I had said that I will come after two days. I always did that. Come uninformed I mean. She found me. But I didn't find what I was looking for. Her eyes didn't shine. She was happy to see me but this wasn't enough to bring a glow to her sinking eyes. They had a haunting look. Like punctured tyres. Hopeless. It hurt. I ran out.

Met friends. We went to the riverside. Ate *pakoras* and had tea. They brought beer too. I didn't have much. "Nausea," I said. "Tomorrow for sure," I told them. "Money on me."

Returned late. Sister opened the door. Her eyes twinkled. But faded too soon. Dim future. Mom and dad had slept. I was a tad disappointed. Normally mom would wait. Though I didn't like their waiting. I felt it was an invasion of my independence. I wanted to be free to eat wherever. I needed to be independent. Dad and I never got along. He wanted a son. I wanted an ATM.

My sister served food. Mom heard the noise of utensils and got up. She sat next to me. She made something I always liked.

"Go and say hi to dad," sister suggested.

I nodded in negative. "It's okay. Meet him in the morning," Mom intervened. She always did. She always let me be. She always understood me. But not quite right. I wanted to see him. But I was afraid. I felt guilty. For not having been able to do anything. Nothing. Here I was, trying to live a life oblivious to their suffering, trying to look over everything, in noise. There they were, living theirs, trying to struggle with everything, in silence. I felt so small. I left for my room and closed the door. Switched off the lights and got into the bed. *Will think about all this tomorrow.* But when do thoughts follow our dictum. What does? *What can I really do? I can't live here. But I can't just let things be like this. I can earn money. But there are things other than money. They need me. What to do?* I brought out the walkman and switched it on. There is nothing music cannot make you forget. Even your conscience.

17
MUMBAI SABKI JAAN: INVESTMENT BANKING

I reached Mumbai. Had barely settled down that the job at Merrill started. The first five days were for training. That was easy. Training was like everywhere else. Informative and boring sessions with frequent breaks for tea and coffee. If only job could be just one, big training, well without the long sessions. More breaks, less talk. I had yet to get awed by the place or people. Had heard so much about it. The most coveted job. The most paying. The most glamorous. Full of mean, money-minded wolves. You have heard all that bullshit I am sure. There are so many people running these banks down these days. Down with them. First they go there, make their money. Then they get out and make money by writing curses about those who are still in there. I had read Monkey Business. Expected everyone to be like one big money-eyed moron. A couple were. But that is true of every place. Why run the whole thing down just to sell your book. Did you say I am taking opposite stance just to sell mine? Hmm...nice catch. Maybe. But the people looked hardly the part, I tell you. Neither dressed nor talked like one. They actually looked more like, well people. *Khalis desi* people. Actually it's not their problem. India is like that. Pizza Hut sells cheese here. Big Mac sells potatoes. Put anything in India and it spoils it by a few degrees. I am an example of it myself! Had it not been for my nationality, I would have been worth a lot more. How much, you say? You sure are an idiot. For you should have asked what my current worth is. Not that I would have answered. How do you calculate what doesn't exist! Anyway, more on self deprecation as a tool for humour later. There are a lot more reasons coming for that. I need to save some tricks for later. Most of these hard-nosed bankers looked like people I had known on campus. Most with specs, seemingly intelligent, focused. Some had great sense of humour. Some were great people. They say war brings out the worst in us. The same is true of banking. It's a tough place. Competitive and grilling. Almost like being on the warfront. No place for errors. So it does turn people a bit rough. But blame it on the business, I say. Spare the people. Most of the other joinees were affable. Looking at them you would never be able to say that they would last long here. But they all do. Almost all. That is how the place is. Even if you feel like *Alice in Wonderland* when you join, very soon you tend to forget the land you came from. I told my apprehensions about being able to last long in the company to one of my seniors there. He looked at me for a while. I doubted if I did the right thing by sharing my doubts. He broke into a loud laughter and took me out for tea. Bankers don't always eat in the fanciest restaurant. You know the old adage; you can take the Texan out of Texas but not the Texas out of him. Or one of its many versions. Anyway, he told me that he thought the same when he had joined. That was five years ago. Every year he tells himself, this will be the last year. And he never keeps the promise. I looked bewildered. He liked my response to him. Patted on my back. "You see, when I joined salary was less so I wanted to leave after two years. "*Would look good on my resume*," I had thought. But after two years, salaries shot up all around. It didn't make sense now. I had just gotten married. My wife complained. But I told her, just two years."

"Then?"

"After two more years my salary shot up even more and now my wife has also stopped complaining. She had gotten used to it like I had." I tried to trace some bit of melancholy-type emotion but there was none. Other than a smile. I wondered if I would like to lose myself like that. *How would it be to stand like him at the tea shop one day with someone younger and narrating the same story?* Didn't look very exciting.

"How long do you plan to stay?" he asked.

"Two years." He sipped his tea. I realized the irony of my statement.

By day three I was pulled out of training. "Why?" I questioned. "I need information too." "You can get that from others. We need you to start working on a deal," told Neeraj, head of the practice.

"Okay."

"Go and meet Rohit. He is your VP on the deal."

"Okay."

I went to see Rohit. There was little talk. It was an IPO of an infrastructure company and I had to handle it all by myself. He would of course be there but on a need to be there basis.

A seat was quickly arranged and I became the proud possessor of a computer which meant I could check mails now. I also had a secretary. *Wow! I should be proud of myself.* But in reality I didn't really like it. *Others are getting two days of fun at training and I have to start working. Heck.*

The next morning I was called to the cabin of senior VP. His job was to manage a relationship on the deal. This meant he met just once a month or something with the promoters, drank fine wine, and discussed women or cricket. No, sorry it was tennis. Actually it depends on what the client likes. He wanted to know if I knew everything about the company I was to do the IPO of or not.

"You did get the data dump last night. Didn't you? I had asked Sujit for that," he asked casually.

I had no clue. *When in doubt do nothing.*

He called up Sujit. "Sujit, did you transfer all the data to Romal? Okay...okay. Good. The file which I gave you two days back? Okay, very well."

"He has transferred all the data. It must have taken you all night to go through it."

"Yes." *If your boss doesn't doubt you, don't give him a reason to.*

"Good. So, now you are ready for Investment Banking."

His heart filled with pride at this word, Investment Banking. My heart sank. *What the devil I have enrolled myself for? I don't even know where Sensex is trading today.* What do you do when your boss doesn't have a doubt? Same trick.

"Yes. I am. If I have any doubt I will come to you."

He didn't look too happy at this response. "Look Romal. I know you are new and it's your first deal. You must be a bit nervous. But that is how we believe the best training is given. Throw the fish in the water and it will learn swimming." *What if I am a, well, lion? Okay, cow? Anything that doesn't like water?*

"Yes sir. I am really kicked about it," I tried to faff.

"Good. Now excuse me. I need to go out for this big meeting today. It's a tough life Romal but believe me it's worth it. Nothing pays more. Welcome to the club." He extended his hand. I shook. I was shaking. Just a bit.

Next morning I was supposed to go for the meeting at the client's. I was waiting at the office for Rohit to join. He came and was surprised to find me there.

"Still here? You must be getting late. The meeting was supposed to start at 9:00. It's already 8:50."

"I...was waiting for you."

"Me? Boss. I am not going to join you there. I have five other deals to look at. Just run right away." I gave him a look. He gave me back. His was sterner. I began to run. I scrambled and collected the documents which I had printed and darted out. I reached a few minutes late. Everyone else, which included the three member team of the competing bank, one domestic lawyer, and one international lawyer were already there. But it was okay. No one had really missed me. We all were waiting for the client's MD. A discussion on the RHP (Red Herring Prospectus) was to happen over the next few days. It was a document which is filed with the regulatory body as part of the IPO process. I had never seen one before. I was supposed to be the one leading its drafting. The client's MD came in an hour late. We all had two rounds of tea and snacks till then. The lawyers came to introduced themselves. After getting my business card, their eyes popped out. I was the banker on the deal. Didn't matter what I looked like. What mattered was what was printed on the card. The international lawyer had an Indian name. But he hardly looked like one. He talked more like a foreigner. He was staying at the Taj President. He was complaining about it. Client's MD came. Discussion began. Everyone tried hard to show that they are adding value. I also tried. To remain seated. I had hardly spoken in the whole day. It had been long since I had done that. It was a milestone achievement. Unfortunately, I was paid for doing just the opposite. I went back to office and blurted in front of Rohit. He listened patiently. I hoped for lots of tips. He gave a couple and told me to read the document and find something. Fish. Water. Pond. Throw. Swim. I had seen the first four. Part five was left on me. I studied all night. Found a few spelling mistakes. Couple of intelligent points as well. Next morning I was ready to burst open. I hadn't slept. I wanted to give my inputs before I doze off.

"I have found a few mistakes in the document," I opened up. They all took notice.

"Yes."

"There is a spelling mistake on page 13…"

"Oh, that's okay. We can discuss that later. The more important thing is…" I lost focus and was completely out of other's focus. Arrgh. I wanted to jump on the table and dance and let them know I am here. All I did was slip in my chair and hide behind my laptop pretending that I was doing something important. How long can you do that? I did for the whole day!

By day three I knew I was in trouble. I had just spoken once in the last two days and everyone had realized my worth. It wasn't much. I was being given a royal ignore. Polite but clear. To add to that I didn't understand the people sitting there. The international lawyer Varunesh had referred *Pakoras* as *stuff* when talking to the client's MD and shown his surprise at the fact that in some parts of India people travelled on top of the train. He acted more surprised than even foreigners do. *There is something I am missing.* The associate girl from the competing bank kept smiling at me. She looked a bit familiar but that was true of all pretty girls I met. She wasn't particularly pretty but still looked familiar. That was curious.

I worked extra hard on the night of day three. But I still remained silent on day 4. I tried a bit but goofed up. I decided to go for a walk after lunch. I was suffocated enough inside. I found Varunesh buying cigarette from the corner shop. I closed in on him.

"Hey."

"Hey."

"You smoke?"

"Nope."

"Mind if I do."

"Nope."

He lit his cigarette. Something lit in my mind. He smoked just like a *Bihari*. Holding it from the middle and sucking hard. *I am missing a lot much more. What is it?*

That night I went out for a movie. How much preparation one needs for keeping mum? After the movie I stood on the marine drive wall. The breeze was doing me good. It brushed my hair. They were short but I still liked the way it ruffled them. *I wish I had shoulder length hair like Sanjay Dutt. It doesn't seem possible anymore. One more thing out of my wish list. Just like Varsha.* Her thoughts were like a desert wind. You like it but it leaves you with dust in the mouth. She had sent an sms today. Apparently she was in town. Her first posting was in Mumbai. "And wasn't I her good friend and won't it be good to catch up?" she had asked. To hell and more. Someone was calling my name I felt. How badly was I missing someone! But no. It kept getting stronger. I looked around. Ah! It was my beloved I-schol Tuchcha! For now I could have done with the company of a bull. He was far better. He was with a friend. They took me to a fancy restaurant. It was post midnight and the café was deserted. Only hard working bankers and consultants are awake at that time. Perks! And one more category. The rich and the ugly. A bald, fat, portly man walked in with two beauties in tow. Together the two had lesser clothes on their entire body than I had on my ass. Actually they had little on the top covered other than their ass. *How do my companions stack up against his?* I gave a quick look. His sizzled. Mine fizzled. Never mind. They say, life is like a Negro's left ball, neither fair nor right. But I think it sucks even if it's like a Negro's right ball. A ball is a ball and that too of a Negro? God!

"What luck?" I said.

"Just work for a few years and it will be same for you, banker," beloved *Tuchcha* spoke, patting my back while his companion placed the order.

"I don't think I would last that long." *And if I do, I would become like the guy holding the two wine bottles, fat and ugly.* I imagined myself in the place of that guy a few years from now. I liked the part wherein my hands were sliding down their bare thighs. Everything else looked disgusting. *Not worth slogging a few years. I want my share right now!* I thought of getting up and introducing myself to the threesome and charming my way into making it a foursome.

"Hey. Which deal you are working on?" *Tuchcha's* friend asked.

"One infrastructure company IPO?"

"What? Are you the guy who sits in the room insolently? Haha."

"What? How do you know?"

"Haha. There is a girl also on the deal. From the other bank…"

"Yes, there is." I remembered the not so pretty girl.

"She is my girlfriend. She is from your insti actually. You shall know her. She is your senior."

"What?" My instincts are not always wrong. Problem is there always is one. I can't trust them.

"Haha. Why don't you talk to her on the phone? Here," he said giving his mobile. I did. Talk to her, I mean. Comforting me, she promised help.

We got up to go. One issue was solved. But the new riddle remained.

Of the bald, ugly, and the beautiful. Still a bit lost, I blankly stood near the table of the two wine bottle girls. The guy was almost into one of them with his hands under her hot pants and mouth over hers. I felt a bit amused and then felt disgusted. I looked at the other one. Thigh upwards. My eyes met her. She was looking straight, away, out of the café, towards the shore. Indifferent to others. Then she turned to look at her friends and gave a short smile. She turned towards me and continued that smile. I tried to give back a knowing smile. Surprisingly we both shared the same feeling. It was disgusting what was going on. I mean my standing there and gawking at them. Her smile shrank and turned into a scorn. *I know what I want, you don't*, it seemed to say. I quickly ran away. I always do. Run away, I mean.

It was Friday and Day 5. Armed with tips from the associate of the competing bank, I made a few points. Not that they were great but she would second my points with, "I agree. That's a good point." I began to second their points with the same, "I agree. That's a good point." Soon everyone including the lawyer knew I had arrived and broken into the club of, "I agree. That's a good point. And here is my point." It was time for everyone to drop their pretence.

"Varunesh, what are your plans for the weekend? Working?" the competing bank's VP asked.

"No. No. *Bilkul Nahin.*" I fell from my chair. *He knows Hindi!!*

"Where did you do your law from?"

"Delhi University. Then went to London for further studies around six years back."

So that was that. He must have known every bit about people sitting on the train and maybe he even sat on it sometime. He not only ate and liked the *pakora* "stuff" but some of his belly fat was owing to that oil.

I came back to the office post 9 pm. There was hardly anyone there. I felt like talking to someone. The office had two parts. I went to the other in search of human life. Parush was sitting there. He was from IIML and expected to be a VP in a year's time. I stood by his cubicle and waited for him to notice. He was busy with some XL file and didn't bother. *Perfect banker. Cares only about spreadsheets and work. Idiot. Moron. Disgusting. Inhuman.* There were a few lines drawn on his desk with some of them struck through. I couldn't help asking.

"Parush, sorry to interrupt, but what are these lines?"

He finally noticed and turned. He had a bright smile. He wasn't so much of a banker after all. "What? Sorry? Give me a minute. I am struggling with this error here."

"Sure." Having nothing else to do, I got involved in his error. Together we debugged it in the next twenty minutes. It is fun working when the responsibility is not yours.

"Yeah. So you were asking something?"

"Sorry?" I had forgotten all about that.

"You were asking something about these lines."

"Oh, yes. Yes. What are these? I mean..."

His eyes lit up. "Make a guess."

"Ummm...I don't know. May be you are counting something. Like days for a vacation or some important meeting or I don't know..." I didn't want to be wrong here.

"Haha. Yes. I am counting days for vacation."

"Oh, yeah?" I had lost interest in it. I was here to talk about myself.

"But of a different kind? A permanent one."

"Sorry? What do you mean?"

"I have promised myself that I would leave this place in the next three years. These are thirty six lines. I strike one after every month you see."

A couple of other people joined us including Neeraj. "Oh, you are discussing his lines and plans. Why are you scaring the young guy?" he said.

"It will never happen Parush, I tell you. This place is like that Eagles song you know," added the other.

"We are programmed to receive.

You can check-out any time you like,

But you can never leave! "

Everyone began to laugh. They had placed bets on whether he will actually be able to leave or not. No matter where you place humans they never leave the human touch even though it may be difficult to see it sometimes. *In this world like everywhere else, nothing is what it seems*, I figured.

Over the weekend I met Varsha. She still had her impact. The dinner was warm. My heart had gone cold. I decided to not meet her again and run as far away as possible. I pushed myself into work. Some GDR deal it was. Like hell I cared. Someone somewhere wants to raise money. What the fuck do I care whether he raises it from India through an IPO or from abroad through GDR. For all I care he can raise it from some lala. Whose life does it change? Other than the one who already has a lot of money. Basically, I didn't care. It didn't look worth the effort. The Friday I got staffed on it, I was planning to go out for a drinking night. I wanted to forget it all. Even if for a while. Like Shahrukh did in *Devdas.*

Kaun kambakht bardasht karane ke liye peeta hai,

Hum to isliye peete hain ki kuchh yaad na rahe

He did it for his *Paro*. I did for mine. He became a star doing that. Sorry. Superstar. What had I become? Loser? Moron? We all have them. *Paros* I mean. And they are just the same. Indifferent to us. Fuck her. I mean in a way of curse not literally. Though that is what you want actually. Hmmm…may be that is why we do not get them. They can see that. Fuck it. Fuck something at least. Fuck whatever or whosoever you wish. I had slogged the whole week to make sure I get the weekend off. I had fucked the life of the representatives of ten banks who were working with me on the infrastructure deal over the week to ensure I am ahead of schedule. But the problem with life is that there is someone above us. I mean God. Not boss. I give a fuck about bosses. Unless they are worth having me. God watches us all the time. In my case he was paying special attention these days. I was a case study. Fuck him. How could I escape while making life of others miserable? What you sow, you reap. In my case he returns the favour immediately. I looked at my watch. It was 7:00 pm. I was ready. I had called up Suman and fixed a meeting at Totos in Bandra. Five more guys were to come. I was beaming. I put my hand on top of my laptop and readied myself to close it. An outlook message popped up.

"New message from Neeraj," it read. *Should I close it and run. If I haven't read the message it wouldn't hurt my conscience if it requires me to stay.* That was the last thing I wanted to do. But there was no easy ways out. *They would ring my mobile. Having the mobile switched off will also not work. It isn't a good enough excuse.* I opened it anyhow. What choice did I have?

"Please meet Manasi. You have been staffed with her," it read. I died. I banged my head on the keyboard. I sensed someone standing over my head. I looked up. I died again. It was Manasi. She was smiling. But I could not see any smile on her face.

"Come on, Romal. We don't make you work that hard. It's okay."

"Ah... no…no. It's not that. Just that…," I fumbled.

"It's okay. Come to my cubicle."

She told me about the deal. We were supposed to be in Chennai on Monday. Before that there were over two hundred pages of material to be read about the company. Its financials for three years and an over fifty page marketing document had to be prepared. A first draft of it had to be ready before we meet them. All this over next two days, Saturday and Sunday. I died. That was my third time in less than thirty minutes. Why have weekends when your week doesn't really end?

"Come on Romal. What is it?"

"What…what happened?"

"You are looking so dead. We don't make life that miserable. Do we? I mean you are making me feel bad about myself."

That was hardly my intention. "No. I mean…I mean I don't know. I am sorry Manasi. Just…just that…I had planned a night out with friends and it suddenly came. So…I mean…you see…it just hasn't sunk in yet."

"*Arre*, okay. So who has asked you to ditch your plan? Just plan it out. Go for it. Don't drink as much you wanted to. Finish it all over next two days. Okay? Happy?"

A faint smile came over me. I saw myself saying no to Suman after my fifth peg.

"No yaar. Have to work tomorrow."

"Hahahaha...Chutia banker," he would say.

It didn't look good. But it was better than saying, "I can't come."

"Have to work tonight. Sorry."

"Asshole you are I tell you," he would have said.

"Okay." I said.

"Now smile a little please. I want you to take the ownership of this deal, Okay? Ask me if needed but I expect you to run the show. Yeah? Now go and paint the town red. Catch you tomorrow."

My smile got bigger. I picked up the reading material and left.

"And we need the first draft by tomorrow evening," I heard her say as I stepped out of her cabin door. It meant no Totos. What could I do? What could she do? Such was the business. Such were not the people. They had a heart. Business didn't.

We were in Chennai. It was good to be out. It gave me a break. We were supposed to be a part of the board meeting. Utkarsh had also come. He was the senior VP and relationship manager on the deal.

"How are you, Romal?" he asked.

"Good Utkarsh."

"Good. Ready for your first board meeting? Excited?"

"Yeah." I didn't know if my eyes will give me away. They didn't.

"Good." He adjusted my tie. "Good."

The board meeting began. Tea and coffee was served. Mineral water bottles were there. Cashew nuts biscuits were there. Something was missing. "*Arre* Shyamu. Don't you have *Krackjack* today?" one of the board members remembered. They are detail oriented people, these board members. After Shyamu left it was turn of the other Shyamu. Me. Manasi indicated to serve our dish to them. Presentation. I hesitated. I was an IIMA graduate. But my training was still to be done. Utkarsh didn't understand the delay. He looked at Manasi. She understood it. She knew me. She wasn't too pleased to know me though. She got up and picked up a few copies and began to distribute. I followed suit. I may not follow orders I don't agree with. But I always follow actions I don't agree with.

Utkarsh made the presentation. He wasn't a very good presenter. His English was poor and rusty. But it didn't matter. What mattered was not how he was. But who he was. He was a banker. From Merrill. That was enough.

After the presentation there was silence. First it looked soothing. The end of the noise brings you peace. Then it began to look prolonged. These board members are people of deep thought. It takes time to do deep thinking.

"So Utkarsh, what is your advice on GDR? Should we go for it?" You see they had understood everything Utkarsh had told them. So no questions on that front. Deep thinkers they were, like I said.

Utkarsh went on for a few more minutes on its advantages. What else could he have said?

"Okay. So what do you all say? Should we go for it?" asked the most detail oriented one. The same guy who had noticed that *Krackjack* was missing.

Everyone raised their hands up. The motion was passed. Everyone looked pleased.

"Shyamu. Bring one more round of tea." It was celebration time after the hard work.

The meeting was over. Shyamu was collecting the cups. I was collecting the presentation.

"Romal, why do you do this?" Manasi asked.

I looked up. Her eyes were tense. And straight on me. And concerned. I knew it was no time for fumbling. *Time to stand up.*

"Manasi. I just don't understand all this."

"What do you not understand Romal? Why don't you like this?"

"Manasi, what is there to like here. I don't get it. I am sorry."

"No. Don't be sorry. It's okay. But I don't understand your not understanding. I mean how old are you?"

"Twenty six. Almost."

"Look. You are so young and you are getting a chance to be part of the board meeting. Doesn't that excite you?"

"It does Manasi. But it dies the moment I see what I am doing. It looks no different than what that guy there is doing. He serves tea. I serve the presentation. What's the big deal?

There was a bit of fire in her eyes. She felt offended.

"Romal. How can you say that? I mean don't look at what you are doing now. Look at what you would be doing five years from now. Look at what I am doing."

"That's what I am looking at Manasi. What are you doing?"

There was a tense silence. She wasn't offended. She was hurt. I won't say fuck it. I cared.

"Romal, I work with CEOs and CFOs. It is so fucking competitive. I mean we are in the middle of this deal and Shittibank is on my neck to throw me out. Fuck. It's so much kickass."

I wasn't impressed. My gaze didn't waver. She got the message.

"What do you want to do otherwise? Consulting? You may like it for a couple of years then all this learning bullshit goes out of the window. You will just end up making two by two metrics. It hardly pays as much."

I stood silent. She got the message. She was talking to herself now. She was answering questions she may have asked herself sometime. I didn't need to say them.

"I agree it's tough to like it here. I mean even I didn't like it initially. But you get used to it. And look at the money Romal. Nothing pays more." She had begun to look somewhere in the middle of us. She wasn't looking at me. She wasn't talking to me. When someone does that, it means they have reached the end of their road. They are looking at a dead end beyond which they have never been able to go. I wanted to look beyond it. It is not the unknown I fear, it is the known I pity.

18

FUCK ME BABY ONE MORE TIME

"A trip to Goa??"

"Yes, over the weekend. Would be fun," said Suman.

I had decided to just work and stay out of everything else. But who wants to miss the fun. *Come Monday and won't I curse myself? May be I can forget myself for sometime there.* Heck.

"Hmmm...let me see if I can manage. You know my job…"

"Yeah…yeah…Mr. Banker. We also work."

"No...no…not that. *theek hai.* Would come. Who all are coming?"

"Some of my Engineering friends, Varsha and…"

Varsha! Hell. Seeing her with her boyfriend may fry my ass again. I shall drop out. But I want to go. How long can I avoid her? Between devil and the deep sea, always choose the deep sea. Devil will follow you there by himself.

The bus trip began on a fun note. Suman had played a trick. He told his Engineering friends that I am a big time stud. That I can tell if a girl is available just by looking at her toe. I dope, booze, and am always ready for the craziest of adventures. He told me the same thing about them.

We remained suspicious of each other during the bus ride and kept throwing knowing, mischievous glances. The first one of them, Chilla, had a funny face. Similar to the comic character *Ghaseetaraam*. Other one, Abhay at first glance looked like a narcissist with his nice, well built body and a baby face. I took the faint smile on his face for smugness. They both worked in the same company. Name? Leave it. How does it matter? They all are same. Aren't they? I remained oblivious to the other two, you know who. They reciprocated and remained locked in their curtain shielded seats. *What's going on in there?* Not a mystery I was interested in. Actually there was no mystery there, just that I was not interested.

The bus stopped somewhere on the way. I stepped out to breathe. The two software studs also alighted. To smoke I figured. Cigarette or dope, I wondered.

They were hovering around me, flashing smiles. I didn't get it. Weird, I thought.

"Do you have a lighter? Or a matchbox?" asked one of the passengers as I shook my head. His face dropped. Feeling sorry for him I added, "Sorry but I don't smoke."

The face of the twin studs lit up and they walked up to me.

"You don't smoke?" they asked in chorus.

"No," I said defensively. To tell dopers that you don't even smoke is a kind of dropping your bravado. Isn't it? But it takes character to stand up and be honest. I tried to console myself.

"Oh. You mean you don't smoke cigarettes?" Again in chorus. More smile flash.

"Oh, no...no. You are getting it wrong. I don't smoke anything. I mean Suman told about you people. Sorry, I can't be part of it." They looked flabbergasted. I explained further. "Oh, but by all means you people continue. I have no issues with it." I still couldn't understand their expressions. It was confusing.

"Are you not carrying dope?" I asked to understand their situation better. They nodded in negative. More confusion.

"Oh, you intend to buy it in Goa. Okay. You should have done some preparation *yaar*."

"Oh, no. Actually we don't..." Abhay tried to reveal something but Chilla quickly chipped in.

"Actually you see we had couple of parties over last two days. So we exhausted it all there." They salvaged their pride.

"Ah." I walked away.

Nothing much happened over the bus journey as we mostly snored. Once there the first day was uneventful. Reaching there we booked hotel rooms. A separate room for them, *you know who*. Arranged for bikes took the afternoon. From then onwards there was speed to us. We roamed around Goa aimlessly on the bikes. What if life could be like this, wandering to nowhere on a speed bike. But without them around, *you know who*. Why am I telling you about them? Forget them.

Chilla, I and Abhay struck a chord once we came to know of each other's reality. We gave Suman a good whole bashing. But it gave us a good idea. What if for the two days that we were here, we posed as someone who doped, boozed heavily, and could tell if a girl was available by well anything. Chilla was sold. Abhay stayed out but found it funny. Suman had lost the right to speak up or say anything on the trip. The other two were not asked. Not that they were missing anything.

Chilla and I tore our t-shirt sleeves, bought 3 goggles each of Rs. 50

and wore it, one on eyes and other two hung from side of our tees. And then there was bandana too for the head. We looked cool. We looked like idiots. But that was so cool.

In the evening we decided to take a ferry ride. As we all came on board, I began to have a problem. Suddenly the two worlds of mine came in close contact and I could no longer look away. The electrons circulating around were now coming close to the nucleus. There were bound to be sparks. I tried to disconnect myself and stood in an empty corner. Suddenly I was getting empty of everything else as well. She stood in the middle of the ferry, happy and dancing. She got wrapped in a pair of arms. Whose, you ask? Fuck yourself, will you.

The ferry waved and wind blew over it. Her skirt fluttered. My heart too. It was all so surreal. The sun was about to set and there was still light though fading fast. Cool, sea wind was there and we all were on a ferry which moved, both ahead and sideways, throwing us out of our comfortable position. We struggled to hold on to ourselves. People were giggling, drinking, and having fun. Sea waves brought water making them wet. They liked it. And in the middle of it all was she. Beautiful she. Mesmerizing she. For a moment the light was only around her. She danced happy and gay, her skirt fluttering. The ferry shook. She bent to hold on to herself and her skirt. More giggles. More merry. Just like a scene out of a movie. Just that it was not a movie. She wasn't even wearing a skirt actually. May be she wasn't even that beautiful. Scenes from life are never as dramatic as in fiction but their impact unfortunately is same or often much worse. Stories have a tidy, neat ending, everything flowing in one smooth coherent style leading to a climax worthy of it to leave you with something. Feeling. Entertainment. Headache. Life is different. There is no clear beginning or ending to it. There is no clear outcome. It depends on your memory, your attitude, and your strength. Basically it depends upon you. It's your responsibility to put a cover on the book of your life and give it a title.

The pages inside have already been filled. I tried doing the same. *It is my life. It is my story. But even in my story she isn't mine. What worth is life?* I tried to look away. Into the sea. It was quite deep. Deep enough for me to drown. *I don't need much water to drown. I am not ready for it. I want someone else to do even that for me.* Fuck whom?

The trip was more or less over for me. But pain lingers long after the accident. We went for dinner. It was a nice place, on the sea beach. Some other time, I would have loved it. Right now all I wanted was to run away. To be anywhere but here. But I had little choice. I tried to escape but couldn't come up with good enough excuses. My new found buddies Chilla and Abhay would not take 'no' for an answer. That's a problem with friends. Sometimes they are not even aware of the damage they are doing. When stars are against you, you begin to see its effect everywhere. I was trying to stay away from *you know who*. But she decided to come and sit close. And she had a reason for it. I looked in a bad mood and she had decided to cheer me up. Friendship, anyone?

"What happened? Why do you look so dead?"

Do I? Really? "Nothing. I am fine. Don't know where you people are getting these ideas from. I guess I am tired after swimming in sea. I become awful once tired." *Excuse. Excuse. Excuse.*

"Is it your job? Is it that bad? Leave it if you hate it so much."

I looked at her and looked away. *It is not about leaving what you hate but getting what you love.*

"What is it? Tell me no. She placed her hand on my arms." Irony. Ah!

"Forget it. It's nothing. Really."

I was looking straight into the sea while she was looking at me. Somehow I could see her expressions without even looking at her. *Or is it just my imagination?* I saw her black, round, shining eyes fixed at me. Mostly in amazement. Like children do when they see a lion or some rare breed monkey for the first time in a zoo. That is how I sometimes felt she saw me.

Just as I began to enjoy her attention even if it was akin to monkey in a zoo or whatever, the other you know who, came into the picture and exerted his rights. By twisting her arms. She wailed and they got busy with each other. The monkey was left to himself. He decided to move somewhere else in the cage. I got up and went towards the beach.

"Where are you going?" asked Chilla. Friend number one.

"I think towards the sea beach. Good idea. Let us also go," said Abhay. Friend number two.

"Okay. Let us all go. It will take some time before food comes." More friends. All of them. *Thank you God. I am so grateful.*

Walking on the beach, obvious things begun to become evident. *It cannot go on like this. I will have to do something about it. Not drowning myself. That I will always need help with. This thing called Luv. It needs to be dealt with.* It was unbearable. It was painful. It was blissful in a strange way. I looked at them. They were still busy. *It is futile. This thing called Luv.*

19

ALL BEGINNINGS HAVE AN ENDING

Angels: Last Meeting

Mentor angel sat in his cabin. Trainee angel knocked on the door.

"Yes. What is it?"

"Sir. It is about the subject of my project?"

"Yes. What about it now?"

"Nothing. Just that I am not feeling good about the whole thing."

Mentor angel frowned, looking up from his pile of files. "Don't worry. It will not affect your appraisal. It's not your fault really. Just a coincidence. It happens sometimes."

"No. I mean, somewhere I have begun to feel guilty."

"Guilty? About what?"

"About the whole thing. I know you would say this is the way things go. And in our kind of job we can't always expect to do good things to people. And that he made a choice himself. But still, can we not just help him in some way?"

"Hmmm...what would you like to do?"

"I don't quite know. May be, may be, just give him some sense of direction."

Mentor angel got up from his desk. He looked out of his cabin window. Steadied his trousers and browsed his beard. "You want to help him?"

"Yes...s..."

"Then just leave him alone."

"What? I don't quite...understand."

He turned towards him. His eyes softened, reverberating with hard earned wisdom. "Everyone thinks humans need us. But that's not the truth. Truth is we need them more than they do. What will we do if they are not there? I have been in this job for long now. And I always wonder if our help really helps them. Or it just...just complicates thing. Messes it up. Like this time. It's always like this. This thing about them, this free will, it always comes in between. It is not we who let their best laid plans go awry. It is they who make us go wrong. All the time. Huh! I just want to retire to some nice beach. And get away from this meaningless job of ours. Someday. Soon enough. Hallejullah to that dear."

"So...what do we do...?"

"Nothing. Just leave him to himself. He will find his way out."

"Okay. I will leave him alone." *I wish I could do a little more.*

Demons: Last meeting

Mentor Demon: "So, what's the news on your subject? How is it going?"

Trainee Demon: "Great. This guy is never gonna make up his mind. I bet on that."

Mentor Demon: "Yeah. Humans are like that. They are idiots. But you better be careful. You know what may happen if he does?"

Trainee Demon: "Whaa...t?

Mentor Demon: "Well, if you give a curse to someone and he finds a way to fight it out then it falls back on you. The person who gave it in the first place."

Trainee Demon: "Noooh? That's not possible. How can that be? We...we are demons. We are powerful."

Mentor Demon: "Yes. But not above universal law. It is like Newton's third principle."

Trainee Demon: "What is that?"

Mentor Demon: "If you throw something at someone and he rebounds it then it comes back to you. Got it?" A sinister smile came to him.

Trainee Demon: "Noooh. You never told me that?"

Mentor Demon: "Didn't I? Well, they don't call us demons for nothing. You can never trust us," he said with glee, rubbing his palms. "It's a game. Come on, enjoy it."

Mentor Demon broke into laughter. Trainee demon was sweating.

The task was cut out now. Luv had to be handled. Something had to be done about home. The job was not working. Or the other two were not letting it work. There was no way to know. Chicken and egg problems have no solution. I couldn't have held on for too long. I had begun to feel like a balloon without gas. Exasperated. One morning I saw a beggar on the road. His life looked so much better. He knew what he has to do the whole day. Nothing. That is exactly what he wanted to do. That is exactly what he will do. Nothing. And what does one need to do nothing. Nothing! So easy. My life was complicated. Or I had made it so. In the day time my bosses would run after me while I would run after my clients, lawyers etc. etc. By evening Miss *You Know Who* will want me. Sms, phone etc. etc. For what? Dinner! Movie! I like them. All of them. But not when the other *You Know Who* is present. I hadn't figured her threesome tendencies earlier. And like all things about her, her threesome was a bit different. It involved just two people. Third one was supposed to observe. I didn't like her taste anymore. I didn't like myself for my taste in her. I hated myself. Haven't I said that enough times? It never sounds enough though.

At night it will be my mom. If she didn't call me, I would. It was strange. I didn't like what she will say nor could I bear her silence. What was she supposed to say! What was I supposed to do! Work front was getting a bit interesting. I could really let you in into a lot more dope on insider story into banking. But I don't want to. Because it is not supposed to be a whistleblower on the banking world. It is my story. I know I have said that too enough times. Bear with me. Please. Don't you see I need you by my side? I got staffed with certain Mr. X whom I had admired ever since my interview with Merrill. He was suave, measured, and composed. He was intelligent and structured too. He was part of the reason I had joined Merrill. I had thought everyone else would be like him or better. But it was not so. They always send their best bet on the campus. Like movie posters always just show the lead stars to make you buy the ticket. Once you are in, you realize that the stars mean nothing without a good script. I was thrilled when he called me to his room. He was tall, lanky, and neatly dressed. There was an aura of cool confidence and *I know I am interesting* around him without any swagger. I liked it. He explained that I needed to prepare a presentation for a company interested in setting up power plants in India. By tomorrow. I had lotsa time. Whole of tonight.

"You will be able to do it. Won't you?"

"Yes. Of course." There was no doubt. But there was in his mind.

He detailed it further. He broke the whole thing piece by piece. Gave me his ideas, told me to fill in the gaps. I was hooked.

"I will see you tomorrow morning at ten." He left. I got busy. Night went just like that. Next day he edited my work. Added some bits. Deleted some. But there was no ill feeling from me. I was too floored. Every word from him sounded like honey. There was hardly any fluff he told. Just cut whatever I had chipped in. There was still work to be done. I hadn't felt happy about work in a long time. I did it. Once. Twice. Thrice. But my face never lost its smile. I slept well after a long time. A job well done can do that to you. Satisfaction of doing it to your standards and your boss' expectations can bring that moment to you. Of contentment. Tomorrow was a big day. A big meeting with the MD of the energy company. Like hell I cared who they were. But I did care about my boss's reaction. That is what I was aiming for. I got up on time. A little too early. Almost at seven. Meeting was at eleven in Bandra. I lived at Marine Drive. I could have left at ten. It was a Saturday. Not much traffic was expected on roads. Still. It was a big meeting. At least for me. I left home by eight. I got a taxi in no time and began chatting with the cab driver. He was from same state as me, UP. But how different had we become. He of open shirt, bare chest and caring two hoots about anything other than traffic. I cared about the same thing. Traffic on the road. Because I had to be on time. Before eleven. I had a formal shirt worth a few thousands on me. Had those rimless specs too. Made you look a bit scholarly and sincere. Not that I liked it that way. But it was important. I looked at myself in the mirror. Looked every bit a banker I say. I smiled at myself. Glanced at the petty taxi driver again. *Worth two cents he is.* But we had similar taste in music. He had his radio station on. The song from *Karan Arjun* played on it. I had loved it when I was in school. Had bunked school to watch the movie with Sudhir. Back home dad was waiting, stick in hand. But it was worth it. Every minute of it. *But what am I doing now? Is it worth a single minute of it?* I looked at the files I carried. The charts and graphs in yellow and blue. It looked a page which was filled with bullshit. It was important. Yes. And intelligent. Very. *What use is intelligence if it doesn't give you the courage to do what you really want. To tell my love that I love her? I really do. If it doesn't set me free to go where I should much rather be. By the side of my parents. In the time they need me.* I looked out of the cab. It stood on the Marine Drive. Waiting for the traffic signal to turn green. *What am I waiting for to jump out?* There were people sitting on the wall along the sea. They were laughing, they were playing, they were frolicking. I didn't know if they had good enough reasons to do so. 'Had they helped someone setup a new energy unit in India in the last two weeks?' I asked to myself. Most likely not. One of the girls on the wall looked at me. 'Not at all!' she said. *Then why the hell do you look so happy? What gives you the right?* The man standing next to her held her face in his palms and turned her towards himself. "Leave that guy to himself," he told her. I turned back and looked at my notes. Then I straightened my tie. *I look neat. I look awesome.* One more look into the mirror. *I look disgusting.* The mirror told me in no uncertain terms. The traffic signal turned green. So did the barometer inside me. I knew it was time to go. To break the cage. To set myself free. I sighed and looked at the cab driver. He was humming the song. *Jaati Hoon Main*... I joined him. It was worth it. Every word of it. *Jaldi*

Hai Kya...There was hurry. Every second counts. Time to do anything is always right now. I was already a bit behind.

The meeting went well. It always does once you have lost interest in it. My mind was long away from the power plants. I said things I understood but didn't care about anymore. I had sailed home. I had already begun to think of the moment when I will hit home. But there were still a few strings attached. I had to take care of them. The cage was open. The pigeon was yet to fly. Something was holding it back. After the meeting I went back to Marine Drive. There was no rain. *Rain, rain, come and drench me. Submerge me. Make me your own. For I am free now.* In my mind I was. It was a matter of time before I would be in reality. I saw some couples walking. Old men. Hawkers. Cabbies. Horse-cart. They all were always there. But I had never noticed them. For I was always somewhere else. Today I was there. Just there. I wanted to be there. Just there. Nowhere else. Soon there will be new cages though. Life is never completely free. Not all the time. You chase a cheese and then it enslaves you. Then you want to run away from it. Sometimes you can.. Sometimes you cannot. I wanted to think about all this later. I wanted to taste freedom while it was there. Thoughts of what is to come are so much more pleasing than the moment when it actually comes. Once it comes you wonder more about what is to follow. Like I was doing right now. For a moment I felt I saw Varsha. The next moment I knew it was just someone else. She was a string I still had to cut loose. I thought of the moment when I would be completely unstringed. "It will entail pruning a few wings of mine," something told me from within. I shivered. Monday, I went to the office. Directly to Neeraj. I told him the news. *I am going.* He looked shocked. He hadn't seen it coming. He tried to know why. I tried to tell. I couldn't. There was so much to be told. So little that could be said. I was going because I had to. How do you explain that to someone? The next few days went in finding words for my feelings. I was made to meet many senior folks.

They tried to convince me to stay. Tried to make me rethink. But I was beyond thinking. I had done enough of it in the last couple of years. They wanted to know why I was going. I wanted to say because I have to. They wanted to know what I wanted. I wanted to say, to be free. Who would have understood that? Who would have approved that? For I didn't approve of it entirely. *Am I going because there was a reason? Or am I just creating a reason because I wanted to go?* Some riddles have no answers really. I never found one. It doesn't matter. It's a waste of time I tell you, these words, these questions and answers. These…you know what I mean. You don't? Then you are like me. I don't as well. High five.

The job was half done. But it is never done till it is done. There is nothing like unfinished business. It's either finished or it is yet to be done. There is nothing in between. I called up Varsha. She had stopped calling ever since I had wanted to talk to her. Strange are the ways of life, man. It sucks. She had heard the news. That I was going. "Why," she asked. "Oh, actually I never told you but I come from an ex-royal family. We used to be very rich and responsible for over forty families who live in the same compound as do I. Post-Independence, government wanted to take our land but we had been contesting against it in the court. My family has just lost the case. My father now needs me by his side. I have to go." *Why I say such ridiculous nonsensical things? Because nothing I am doing is making any sense anyway,* came the answer. *I am doing what I am doing because that is what I have to do. How will you explain that to her?* Strangely she appeared to believe it. I could see her wide eyed expression even over the phone. *It must be looking like one big exciting story. Amusement?* I didn't care. I hardly cared about anything anymore. I had tasted freedom. I wanted more of it. From myself. From my confusions. From my desires. From my conflicts. We decided to meet up. A date was fixed. I looked forward to it. I really did.

20

AND IN THE END NOTHING MATTERS

There she was, standing by the sea shore, the queen's necklace. *She is my queen and if she agrees I would spend the rest of my life finding a necklace worthy enough of her.* Dressed in a black *kurti* with some strange embroidery, she looked quite something. My mind didn't have a word for what she looked like, but my heart was responding to it. I could hear it beat faster. Coming near I stood at a little distance, unsure of how to bring my presence to her knowledge. She suddenly turned, flashed that smile and brought the expression she normally had on seeing me. An expression I never quite understood. I didn't know what it meant. *Interest, curiosity, liking? Love??* Today was the day to find out. Whatever it was, I wasn't prepared for it. Some things you cannot be prepared for, no matter what. Coming close she gave a hug. I stiffened and realized one more thing. I keep realizing something all the time. It's not worth a penny I tell you. It wasn't about that *kurti* or whatever she got dressed in, it was just her smile which did for me. And those eyes; round, black and lost at me.

"Pizzeria?" she asked.

"Yes, sure." *Whatever.*

She walked ahead. I kept looking at her body outlined out of her dress. Her waist was covered but I knew there is a wide birth mark there, somehow I could see it. I had one too. There was sea breeze but it was doing nothing to put me to ease. Nothing could have.

"Sorry, I couldn't meet you earlier. When are you leaving?"

"Tomorrow. Tomorrow afternoon is the flight."

"Oh, I won't be able to see you off. Office."

"I know. That's all right. You came for the dinner, that is good enough."

The waiter approached and we quickly placed an order. Silence filled the space. An awkwardness built inside. Something was bursting.

"You know, I called you for something."

No response. Just a blank look of those eyes that I never understood. *Interest, curiosity, liking? Love??*

"I mean, nothing special. It is rather a very ordinary thing, you know. Everyone goes through…" *What the heck.*

Blank look. *Curiosity?*

"Okay, let me try to cut it short and come to the point. But don't interrupt in between. Okay?"

Head nod. *Eyes have something in them. Does she know? Aren't girls supposed to be perceptive?*

"I guess you know what I am going to say. Don't you?"

Head nod. Negative. *What the hell. Who is dumb here?*

"Okay. Here it goes." *No more uu…umm… please!* "It has been a long time since when I have liked you. I knew it all along but kept running away. But I can't run anymore. I can't. I just want to say that…I like you." *I like you. I like you. I like you a lot. I will die irrespective of whatever you say. I will. I already feel so…so…well…whatever.*

Face still blank. Eyes still shining but no hint of an expression. *God, what is it?*

"You are not joking, like you always do? Are you?"

I could see how my fooling around with myself had fooled everyone else as well. I was a master clown. I nodded my head. Sideways. She still remained silent. Eyes on me. Then down in the plate. Then away.

"Okay, see I didn't want to make you uncomfortable and I don't even expect an answer. I somewhere know what your answer will be. But I do not want to live any further knowing that you don't know anything about how I feel about you."

"No. I will give you an answer. You deserve it."

It was my turn to go blank. "Didn't you see it coming? Did you not know?"

"Just vaguely. I felt so a couple of times but then I was never so sure."

And would being sure have made any difference? Could I have done anything to change this moment?

"I know we have a connection. We get along very well. But am sorry, I never thought of you that way. I always thought we could have been good friends, but that's what it is."

Her eyes were still the same to me. Inscrutable. But I could see the brain behind it better. I didn't have much disk space there.

Rest half an hour went in about that much time but it looked somewhere between zero to infinity. I had no sense of time. We ate in silence. I could hear chatter and voices of world around with absolute clarity. The world inside stood still.

We stepped out of the restaurant and the breeze touched again. I wanted to cry but time for that hadn't yet come. I had to collect more reasons.

"We should go. We can get taxis from the other side of the road."

"No. Let's sit on the Marine Drive for a while," she insisted. *Can I say no!?*

The silence was no more a friend. It was a demon that must be killed. There was no music left in me. I had to let the noise come out. It will do the trick. Even if for a while only.

"You know, you know. Why can't we be more than friends? I really like you a lot. I…I can't live without you. You won't know but when I see you everything in me dies other than you. I can't imagine a life without you. Why…why did it happen? I won't be able to deal with it. How could you not see it earlier? Didn't you see it in my eyes…?" I blurted with my head down. I looked up to find her eyes fixed at me. They had more keenness in them than ever but they still were blank to me. And still very pretty.

"You will manage. I know. You will meet someone. Someone better."

There is no one better. There cannot be. I don't want to meet someone else. Why not you? I didn't want to say anything further. Words were futile I knew. The silence was unbearable. So was the noise now. What was it that I could bear?

"Let us go." She stood up and waved towards a taxi. I watched her negotiate with the driver. She gave me a quick look and sat into it. Patience is a virtue I didn't have it. *What is the virtue I have? Friends? Let me use them. Let me go and get drunk and turn it into a brave story of a kid who did what he was afraid of. To confess his weakness, his love and got a no and was laughing. Won't it make a brave picture? Or may be a dramatic one. Of one who lost but is still laughing. Yes, it shall work.* I called for a taxi.

I heard her call. Stepping out of her cab she walked towards me. *Change of mind? No money for taxi? Forgot something with me? Love?? Fuck it.*

She hugged tightly. I couldn't stiffen up and hugged back.

"Keep in touch. Call me or mail me."

"Sure." She left. I left.

"How did it go?" Suman asked. The waiter came. "Kingfishers?"

"No. Howards today. Strong." Smile. Grin. "I did it."

"You told her."

"Yes." Wide grin. *It is working.*

"What did she say?"

"Usual."

"Good friends?"

"Yeah." Laugh. *Working well. I knew it.*

"Snacks."

"Yes. Chicken."

"Non-veg?" mild surprise.

"Yes. Time to break rules. I just got my heart broken." More laughter. It was great. *Whatay dialogue. Whatay drama. It is working.*

Joint laughter. "Whatay ass you are." More laughter. We laughed together. I fizzled out. *Who am I fooling? It isn't working.* He kept on laughing. His head bent backwards.

Pretended headache. Asked for the bill.

"What happened?"

"Nothing. Just remembered that I am yet to do the packing for tomorrow. Need to leave you now."

"Just one more."

"You have. I won't. Feeling terrible."

"You are not feeling senti because of…?"

"Come on!!!" He couldn't see my hurt. I wouldn't admit. Paid the bill and left. Reached home by 1:00 am. Packing was over in fifteen. A lot of time was left. A whole lifetime. Could just about manage till the flight time.

Flight time was far away. Tomorrow. The time in between looked more than a few hours. It looked forever. Couldn't stay at home. Took a taxi to Marine Drive. Wanted to feel her presence. Presence of the moments had witnessed a little while ago. Still had to begin believing whatever all had happened. Was free but wasn't feeling like that. Free I mean. *Have done what had set out to. Done with everything in the "To Do" list. Have nothing left on the agenda. Nothing on the mind atleast. Why is it not at peace still? Mind I mean. Why is it pre-occupied? What is churning inside?* Slowly a pattern began to emerge in the stormy thought process. A few shapes here and there. The lucky chance. Entry into IIMs. The troubles at home. My strange love for Varsha. Sinking and futile. My constant efforts at running away. Hope of reaching an end from where could script a different story of the past. My constant and miserable failures. At summer placement. At final interviews. The sham that it was, the I-schol status I mean. My intense churning at finding the purpose of my life. Finding out something which I could do nothing about. Friends, the good and the bad ones, moments, the sweet and the sour ones, dreams, the fulfilled and the unfulfilled ones. All came back to hound. All had changed now. So had their colour. Coloured with today's reality, they were becoming like today. Brittle and hollow. A huge turmoil arose. My misery had begun to get names, places, instances. Eyes began to black out. Could sense something but couldn't fathom. Scared, looked for company. There were many people on the road but none looked comforting. Called for a taxi. "Juhu Chowpati." It sped. Kept looking out anxiously. Kept fidgeting nervously. A monster was gnawing. A wave was approaching. Wanted to be near the sea before they took over. Wanted to gain the comfort of the old, mighty, alive sea. Restless from within, calm on the surface. Just like me. Ran towards the beach. Got down from the taxi. Wanted to get lost in the crowd. *They won't be able to find me there. Can hide among the others like me. The ordinary. The common.* Not quite so. Could sense them everywhere I went. Their waiting eyes. Their lusty mouth. Wet with saliva waiting for meat. My meat. The huge wave standing above. Waiting for me to stand still. For it to crash. On Me. "How long can we play this game of hide and seek?" I asked myself. "As long as we can," it told me. The place was getting deserted. Couldn't bear it any longer. *Let it happen. Let it crash. On Me? Let them feast. On Me? It is draining me out anyway. Would die of exhaustion in a little while anyway. Of what worth is life? To what end, for what purpose?* Looked for, found and reached a lonely deserted corner. *If it has to happen, may it happen in peace.* Closed my eyes. Waited for them. To come. To jump on me. To feast on me. But they didn't. Come I mean. No one came. Someone went out instead. The beast. The beast had jumped out. *He is deserting me in my hour of need? He is deserting knowing am weak and listless? Knowing that it would further debilitate me? Of course! What benefit would he have now by remaining with me? He is a man of action. Quick thinking, opportunistic, and agile. He has made his move. He had to. Make his move, I mean.* There was nothing I could do. Other than stand and watch. Like a spectator. Had I not been a spectator all along? Laughing at my own misery? Clapping at my own defeats? Weakness spread throughout my body. Then he fell down. The poet. "Et tu poet?" I asked teary eyed. He didn't say anything. Just moved away. Making me hollow. Making me empty. I had no strength. Not even to kill myself. The sea was but a few feet away. Had no strength to carry myself to it. Shaken to the core was I by the poet's desertion. *Him of all people! Him, whom I always thought to be gentle, friendly, and sage! I have begun to understand the world now. Everyone here is with a purpose. With an agenda. No one comes to you for nothing. No one lives with you for you. They do so for what they can get from you. When they do not get what they want, they leave you. Like he had. The poet.* And then he moved out. The philosopher. Quietly, with measured, small steps. *He is moving like I won't notice! I don't like him. But at the moment I could have done with him as well. He should have stood by me even though I throw barbs at him. What could I have done? He always served a bitter medicine. He never understood my point of view. He always told his. Point of view I mean. He, the wise. He, the mature. He always made me feel small. I was never quite able to see him in the eye. But today it is different. Today I can see anyone in the eye. For today, I can see with all my honesty that I have done no wrong. I have been wronged. By everyone. By the world. The people. The destiny. By my courtiers.* I had gone numb. My eyes were lifeless. I looked at them. The others. They didn't have it in them to look at me. They knew they were guilty. They had wronged me. Me, the wronged me. The beast had gone closer to the sea. The poet was sitting in the shadows. The philosopher had moved away leaving behind the footprints fast being eroded by the sea-wind. I was alone with nothing. Was nothing. Felt nothing. And then it came. The emotion. Like a backlash. Like a reverse tide wanting to purge itself out. I crashed on the ground holding my chest. Feeling a deep throbbing pain. The pent up emotions were trying to find a way out of my heart. Fearing an heart attack, I held my chest tight. It found another way. It came out of my mouth. I puked. Couldn't hold the dark, ugly turbulent mass inside me anymore. It was coming out of every place possible. Tears had begun to dry with the loud, incessant cries. The hollow vessel of my heart churned but there was nothing left to throw. I looked for someone to come for rescue. No one came. The ever so self-reliant proud me asking for help! But the help didn't come. I remembered the one who had always helped me. The Master. A semblance of hope flickered. "He would come," it said. "Sooner or later, he would come. You just have to survive. You just have to keep breathing," it kept saying. The hope, I mean. It comforted me. Tears began to come now. I sobbed in a way I had never known before. The animal I had sensed earlier was doing what I had sensed it might do. Tearing me apart. With its long, sharp claws, ripping my inner corridors, making space to come out. Finally it did come out. Leaving me to fend for myself. Coughing, shivering, and convulsing. Desolate and bleeding. But the Master didn't come. And the tears couldn't come. Making me beyond desolate. Beyond everything. Like a dried mass of wood. Twisted and scarred. Forever. Like a broken glass. Hurt and wanting to hurt. Like spilled water. It may be gathered together but dust would meld in. I lay like a pathetic piece of shit. I don't know how long I was there for. Time didn't matter. Nothing mattered anymore for that matter. How many times would I say that! And then deserted the last standing self of mine. The observer, I mean.

Darkness was there. The dawn was far. I could breathe now. I could observe. "So that is still with me. The observer, I mean," I observed. My only companion. A dull and disturbing companion. It never leaves you. True. It never lets you be in peace. Equally true. It keeps taking notes. Keeps telling you of things, irrespective of whether you want to listen or not. Irrespective of whether you like what it is telling or not. There was nothing good to take notes of. It made my misery even more acute, by constantly making me aware of it. I looked for the tricks which comforted me in the past. *Proximity to the sea?* Gathering myself I moved closer. To the sea I mean. Its water touching my feet. But just the skin. Couldn't touch me any deeper. Sat amidst it. The waves came and crashed. They tried to cajole, they tried to cheer. But to no avail. They stopped trying and left me alone. I kept sitting. With myself. Began to miss my irritant courtiers. Desperate was my loneliness. I looked back. They sat huddled together. The courtiers I mean. *Hadn't they left? And where is the Master? Why didn't he come to my help? Why didn't he come to comfort me?* I didn't understand it. I understood nobody. Not even myself. Didn't want to. Understand I mean. Wanted to move away from everyone. Including myself. The me I knew. The me I liked. Wanted to turn my back on every reminder of the past. I wanted to become a new me. A new self that old self would not be able to recognize. Would not be able to know. If ever the two meet by chance, they shall pass each other like strangers. It shall have no shadow of my past misery. The new self, I mean. For it was a suffocating burden of memories I had. I turned deeper into the sea. Wanting to test myself against the tide. Wanting to see if the fear of death, the scare of drowning will bring any sensation to my numb self. Stood neck deep. Waves came and submerged. I withstood them. The stubborn me. The dried wood still had its innate strength. The broken glass still had its sharpness. Spilled water doesn't lose its flow. It is not flowing. As long as it is not flowing. Came a mighty one. Wave, I mean. Larger than anything I had seen. Mightier than anything I had withstood. I stood still. Fearless. Emotionless. Looked at it with still, stiff eyes. It stood towering before crashing down. Uprooting me. Throwing me. On the beach, away from stones, in the comfort of sand. Rolled over a few times, slowly coming to halt. Some other moment, some other time, would have jumped with joy. Would have giggled like a baby. Not this moment. Not this time. Felt something had never felt before. A sensation I had never known. Felt being cut from within. A knife was plunged in my icy self. No blood spilled. A searing sensation, not of joy. Of someone twisting me from within. Making my whole body feel the pain. That was it.

The pain. Pain is what I felt. It was not a new feeling. Had felt it before. Felt constantly its sizzle. Kept constantly running away. Never faced it. Never gave in. We were still strangers. Pain and I, I mean. It was a different pain this time. It brought me satisfaction. I didn't resent it. I looked forward to it. Had turned against myself. Didn't want to bring joy to myself. Didn't want to heal. Wanting to bring pain to myself. Making myself suffer. That was my thing now. That was my goal. Pulled myself together to go into the sea again. To test myself again. *What do I have to lose anymore? What is it that I expect to gain? Nothing.* Looked with a smirk at my erstwhile courtiers. They had a quizzical look on their face. Like they didn't understand what I was doing. Why I was doing whatever I was doing. Enjoyed it. Enjoyed bringing pain to them. Wanting to be noticed. Wanting my presence to be acknowledged. Wanting them to live in the knowledge of my suffering. Knowing they are responsible for it. They brought it on me. By deserting me. Secretly wanting them to come. To stop me from doing what I was doing. Moved deeper into the sea. The sea deeper into me. A few street kids frolicking in water. Looking at them grew envious of them. *They are better off than me.* They never had to lose. They never had anything. They never have a sense of loss. They never desire anything. They can dance, be happy and carefree. Just keep splashing water upon each other. It's their birth right. To be happy, I mean. Their happy giggles made me aware of my silent misery. Went deeper in, looking for a corner. Lonely, desolate and dark corner. Where no one would want to come. No one would want to go. Where I could hide and cringe. Wishing someone came. Wishing someone pulled me out. It was difficult to find. Such a corner, I mean. *Had never let such a corner exist. Had never let any bit of me remain in shadows. It all had always sparkled under the sunshine. Radiant and bright. Effusive and alive.* I kept looking. Through the cluttered mess. Through the scattered self of mine. Till I stumbled upon something. A new tiny atom. Exploding somewhere within me. Where had it come from? Something strange, something divine, something noble. "Was I really suffering alone?" it made me ask. "Were they not suffering with me? My courtiers. Did they really desert me because they realized I was of no use? Or because they were hurt themselves and couldn't take it anymore? Just like me. Did they also need time to recover? Just like I need? Were they also like me? Human and weak. Did they also not need what I needed? Love and compassion. How often did I give that to them? How often have I asked them what do they need? Ever? Never?" A tiny tear formed near the corner my eye. Quickly rubbed it off. *It is just my fancy. They are selfish and wrong. But what if they are not? Did I enquire? Did I notice?* Couldn't say yes. A secret wish began to germinate. For them to have suffered. For my suspicion to be true. That they deserted me out of their own hurt and weakness. Not because of my fall. It was my last window to my old self. A wave approached. Didn't turn away. Hadn't decided upon whether they were guilty or not. Threw me back on the beach. Rolled, gathered, and stood up. Turned towards them. Watched with keenness. They were constantly looking at me. My courtiers, I mean. Felt a weak, faint smile on the poet's face. Took a few steps towards them. The poet stood up. Moved a step ahead. The beast yawned. Looked at me with disinterested eyes. The philosopher remained still. Could see something on the poet's neck. Marks. Like scratches. He was hurt too. Like me. He too was suffering. Like me. Had lost his inspiration. Had lost his love. Had lost his lofty goals and ideals. Like me. He too felt punished for being virtuous. For being honest. For being forthright. For being right. *A handful of his marks are visible. Must be having many more on back and chest.* He never complained. He never blamed. He never criticized. He was waiting patiently. Such a large hearted person he is. The poet I mean. I began to understand him now. Moved closer. Folded my hands. He held them amidst his. Warm, thin and shaky. Giving me the kind of forgiveness only large hearted poets can. The one which is not even acknowledged. The one which is not even recognized. Neither in words, nor in thoughts. It can happen only when two people become one. *He was always mine. But when was I his?* Looked at the beast. He was bleeding. He had been injured. He had suffered. His eyes had dimmed. Looked dull and rusty. His idea of self had been shaken. His eyes had lost their fierceness. Had witnessed more defeats than he could take. At the hands of Varsha. At the hands of interviewers. At the hands of ever so fickle and changing me. At the hands of the fate. Making him cut short his ambition. Making him chose a path he didn't want to take. His spirit had been tamed. *What is he without it? Just a huge bulky animal with a canine tooth. Where would he get the will to pierce them into someone? Where will he derive his strength to believe that he does what he wants and he gets what he sets out to get. For he has lost far too many times now. At a time like this, when he needed me the most, I had turned against him? I, his master. I, his constant companion. I his source of inspiration. How very selfish of me.* Ruffled his back. Lying on my feet he licked. My feet I mean. Tears began to well. Began to feel like my old self again. There were still a few knots. Still a few hurts. *What about the philosopher? What use has he been of? How has he suffered?* He was still an asshole to me. "Isn't he just a worthless piece of me," I asked. To myself "He has the courage to speak the truth to you. It is no mean feat to speak the ugly truth to you. To say what you never want to hear. To say what is against your wishes," came the answer. From myself. It is right. It is no mean feat. To say it to the rude me. The arrogant me. The haughty me. What had I done to him in return? Rebuffed him, mocked him, secluded him. Didn't I make him feel alone, neglected and misused? Wasn't I guilty of constantly bringing suffering and misery to him? What right did I have to accuse others when I myself have brought so much misery on me? I didn't know how to apologize to him. I wanted to hug him. Tug at him. But he was emotionless. I didn't know how to deal with such people. The know it all, always the same, motionless fellow. I didn't understand one tiny bit. Of him. But he did He understood every tiny bit. Of me. Faint glint of approval came to his eyes. "I understand that you have understood," it said. He understood that I didn't know how to reach out to him. He knew that I am too proud a child to openly apologize. He let it be so. He considered it said without even my having said it. He, the ever so graceful. He, ever so knowledgeable. Felt guilty of having used them. Having exploited them. All of them. For furthering my own shallow agendas. Me, the fickle me. Me, the no me. Me, the ordinary me. How very ordinary had I become under the garb of my ordinariness? It all began to get swept away. All the guilt. All the past. All the unfulfilled future. Everything of me that had ever been, in reality or in imagination. It all began to desert me. Didn't stop it from happening. Let it be. Behind it all, unperturbed by it all, untouched by it all, had begun to sense a new me. The me, had never seen before. The me, had never met before. The me, had never imagined before. Felt awakened. Dawn was still far but wasn't waiting for it anymore. Something was still puzzling. *Where is the Master? If I have been wrong in understanding the intentions of my courtiers then so must have I been in understanding his. The Master. Why didn't he come? Where is he? Why is he still hiding?* Could sense that he is somewhere close. Could tell he is watching. But couldn't tell why is he not showing himself up. *What is he waiting for?* And understood that too. In that strange moment of enlightenment everything occurred like pieces in a jigsaw puzzle.

He didn't come because he didn't want to help. He didn't come because he knew that the time to seek his help was over. Time had come to find my own answers. For he knew that I am going to suffer. And he wanted me to suffer. For he knew my sufferings would not be over till I have suffered completely. He knew that I may get washed away by my suffering. But he kept hope. A nervous, anxious hope. Hope against hope. He wanted me to make this journey back to myself alone.

He knew that I would reach a point from where I could turn towards anything. To any direction. To anyone. He knew that I would be right in whatever choice I make. For I was right in my turning against myself. I had been wronged. There was no denying that. He knew that he cannot win in an argument today. Not anymore. He knew that his guidance had not brought what he had promised. He knew that it was not his fault but the blame was still his. He knew all that. And he wanted me to make that choice by myself. To witness that point. Live that point. Find my own reasons to come back. If I do.

I could choose to move away. Move away from the past I knew. Move away into a future I never knew. That would have been my choice. And he had to live with that. He may or may not have joined on that path. That would be his choice. I would have had to live with that. Or I could come back. Come back to my locii which I was always running away from.

Was I not looking in others what I should have looked within me? Wasn't my love for Varsha flawed for it came with an expectation that only I could have fulfilled? Was it not right for fate to do it to me? May be or maybe not. May be I am just rationalizing it all. To cover the hurt I had undergone. The hurt which I had long been running away from. Defeats which I had for long not accepted as real. But it didn't look like that anymore. For the first time ever I could hear no doubting voice when I made a statement. I began to feel that that it was all for a purpose. It was all to make me learn what I never wanted to. Make me see what I could have never seen through others. It may not be of great value, but it looked like the only thing of value. This, this finding, this resurrection, this new found meaning, a new found self. A wry smile surfaced as I realized how I had become what I always mocked. A philosopher. I always pitied him and today I had begun to talk like him. Was he not just a mirror image of something within? Ah, I soon become like whosoever I pity. So friends, if you ever have felt pitied by me, fikar not. I shall soon be what I thought you to be. Now that I had everything, I began to look for what would prove that I am right. The Master. *If I am right in understanding his intentions, if I am right in interpreting the meaning behind the whole catharsis then he must appear now. He must make himself visible. If he doesn't then I shall turn back into the sea and drown myself. For I would know I have been right all along and all my courtiers and the Master were the selfish deserters.* And lo, he appeared. He was sitting right in front of me on a tall sand tower. Watching me all along. Waiting for me to reach my loci. A smile broke on everyone's face. Me, the Master, and my courtiers. Nee, my brothers. My band of brothers. They are no more separate, they are no more different. *What am I without them? And what am I not when with them?* Me, the mighty me. Me, the rapturous me. Me, the thundering me. *Who in the world will be able to stop me when I charge down with my band of brothers? Laced with the large hearted poet, guided by the wisdom of the philosopher, and lead by the fiery beast. Nobody I say.* The beast transformed into a large mountain wolf. Gave a loud roar and ran into the distance along the beach. The beach shook with his thunderous movements. The poet's wounds had begun to dry. He played with the street kids in the water. The philosopher stood smiling before he went for a walk along the beach. I moved towards the Master and sat beside him. He kept looking straight. Looked at his calm, placid face and began looking towards the sea myself. Then, like a Karan Johar movie came the sunrise. Bollywood is in my genes I tell you. Nothing can take it away I tell you. It really happened. Am not kidding. I kept my hand on his. The Master's I mean. Not Karan Johar's. I like him but I can't trust him. You know what I mean. It had hardened. The Master's hand I mean. Not Karan Johar's you know what I mean. Blisters on his hand had burst. His face had wrinkles. He was growing old. I was growing up.

Things became a little easy after that. Am back home now. Looking after dad and his business. But they never quite become easier. Things, I mean. Life is a struggle, all right. The promise I made to myself that day on the beach, the knowledge that I made this decision to come back myself, makes it easier. My days are harrowed, charred by flashes of the past, of what could have been but couldn't be but nights are peaceful. Had a settlement with the angel and the demon. Have never had a disturbed sleep since then. For a few months may be. It was horrible to begin with really. It is one thing to decide to do something and quite another to actually do it. Didn't want to tell you that but had too. Would have liked to maintain the dramatic value, the heroic quotient of the moment I have created above. But that would be a lie. Decisions can be made out of emotions, out of heightened moments, but to live them through needs mental commitment. Emotions fizzle, lose their sheen, get lost in the clutter. Thoughts remain. Lingering in mental space, coming forth like a warning light every time you astray. And I couldn't astray for I had made a promise. To honour my commitments. To stand by my promise to myself. For that single promise I had had to honour many others. Promises I mean. To face the truth. To state the truth. Every day. Every moment. The bare truth, the ugly truth, the harsh truth, the uplifting truth. Not that I am always successful at it. I err too. We all do. Sometimes the emotions get too strong. The ugly side of the truth gets too heavy to bear. The perspective I build, I see and others don't, sometimes doesn't find a link. The chain is broken. Leaving me stray. Like a boat lost in the sea. I go and relieve myself. By whatever way possible. Like I did once. By calling her up again. Varsha I mean. Couldn't hold it. Had to try again. Had to face the ugly truth again. That she is not so much into me. The movie with that name has come now but I had been living it for long. And then I met her again. Didn't say anything to her this time but waited for her to say. Something. Anything. She did say. But nothing of real value. I was of hardly any value to her. She still hadn't begun to see me. Just as I could never see her. The real her. It had stayed futile. This thing called Luv. I came back home. Valueless, worthless, pointless. Then the morning happened. A new dawn. Dawn renews me. For it brings a new question, a new doubt, a new riddle. Did I do the right thing for myself? The whole day, going through the various to-do's I keep searching for the answer. For am not able to sleep, till I find it. And then I do. Find the answer I mean. Just around the dawn. But slowly it all eased out. It always does. That's what I hate about the whole thing. No matter how intense, feelings do not last. You can not trust them. They say do this else you will die. I do and still die. Then I see haven't really died. I'm alive. They tell the truth but only of the moment. If you don't cross the moment, it remains. Crossing it, begin to see many truths. Sometimes, more than what would want to see.

Enough footage to the philosopher in me. I still have trouble with him. His truths keep getting harsher and harsher. But now we have learned to live together. Me and my band of brothers. We do have squabbles. Healthy ones. Like it happens in every family. Even in Karan Johar ones. The tide began to turn. It always does. Fortune began to favour me again. Had always been its favourite child. The trainee angel quit his internship and joined me. He is my business partner. Son of my father's business partner. He is nice. How can a creep's son be so nice? Must be the angel's doing. It was partly his fault to begin with. Brought a pet dog. It's called devil. It's big and burly but stays very calm with me around. I pour water on it every night as revenge. It never says anything. It knows what it is paying for. So, life is great. What? Oh, love. Ah, this is mysterious. And also futile. This thing unnecessary called Luv. As per Mirza Ghalib,

"Mohabbat mein pharak nahin hai jeene aur marane mein
Ki usi ko dekh kar jeete hain ki jis jalim pe dam nikale"

He was a great *shayar*. Must be true what he said. I feel so. Enough aid.

EPILOGUE

The prologue was fictional, but the story true.